At the age of sixty-eight, Steven Ribman becomes driven to write a novel, a first. His worn image in the mirror, his flagging energy, and those fleeting, but uncomfortable, body sensations are reminders of his own mortality. He envisions his book will be a means to express ideas he has never shared, a record of memories that are disappearing, memories that define who he is. He sees his book as a document to leave behind that speaks of him more eloquently than a grave marker.

Faced with a sheet of blank paper, Steven realizes that he lacks the essential elements for the sweep of a novel: a story category, a structure for the message he wants to convey, characters appropriate for the emotions, conflicts, and reactions that he feels are the heart of his narrative.

Believed by Steven to be good fortune, the events of one night's dream provide him with a starting point for a narrative to build upon. A woman in the dream, Bernice, introduces herself and reveals that she is aware of his attempt to compose something significant. He finds her strangely inspiring and motivating; her suggestions for a story line ignite the fires of creation within him. Strangely, the dreams occur often; the woman reappears each time. Through the force of her ideas and her coaching, the draft of his novel takes shape. Each chapter becomes a tale of their talks and their travels.

Although he is grateful for the progress in his narration and for the return of his enthusiasm for the project, he is troubled to discover he has become increasingly dependent on her guidance. Steven observes a growing relationship at each dream liaison. More disturbing is the recognition that he, a man with a gratifying marriage to Evelyn, has acquired a physical attraction for Bernice that occupies more and more of his waking hours.

The dreams become addictive departures from his waking life. They grow longer, more involved, and more intense. His book, as it evolves, becomes a diary of a life he has never lived. Steven finds himself questioning what is real and what he has dreamed. And who is this woman he discovers had connections with his father, who has taken control of him?

LONG CONVERSATIONS, OLD REGRETS

Also, by William Vietinghoff

The Interceptor Program

This Island Santa Susana

The Moon by June

LONG CONVERSATIONS, OLD REGRETS

BY WILLIAM VIETINGHOFF

> I think we dream so we don't have to be apart so long. If we're in each other's dreams, we can play together all night.
>
> William Watterson – *Calvin and Hobbes*

THOUSAND OAKS, CALIFORNIA

WRITERS ANNEX

For information contact the publisher at
willvee@writersannex.com

ISBN-13: 978-0-578-67019-5

Library of Congress Control Number: 2020936046

Book design by Writers Annex™
Cover design by Writers Annex™

First Edition 2020

To Erick and Craig,
who have their own ways with words

STORY ONE

THE BOOK

THE corner of the garage where Steve probed the shelves was the darkest and dustiest. He shoved aside worn corrugated cardboard cartons overflowing with unidentifiable coils of abrasive brown rope, lengths of dark plastic tubing, and glass jelly jars with scratched, checker-patterned lids that should have been thrown out years ago.

The place had become a museum. Where was the damn box? The objects arrayed around him each had a reason for being there, each tied to an event in his life—events, he was discovering, that could not be recalled too clearly. And that failure to recall was discomforting.

He was certain he had pushed a box of printer paper onto one of the shelves a month ago—or did he? He didn't want to accept that his memory was failing him that badly. You don't lose a whole box of paper for God's sake. The lack of knowing where he put it angered him. In the last month memories had become very important to him. He had earned them; he needed all of them. But too many things, like the printer paper, were going astray in the house.

Four weeks ago, his preoccupation with the front page of the morning newspaper waned and he casually turned to the obituaries—something he usually avoided. There, in small font, were the condensed biographies and praises for men and women he did not know. He looked at the stamp-size portraits of the deceased. He imagined *his* features there. Which of the few decent photographs taken of him recently, showing him timeworn and weathered, will be chosen? But then it might be more flattering to include, as was often done, a photo of him as a good-looking young serviceman in his sailor suit, the dress blues with the snow-white cap square on his head, per regulations.

What will the words be under *his* photograph? He couldn't imagine his life's story being condensed into a couple of paragraphs. It was at that moment, with a vision of, maybe, a fifty-word eulogy, that he knew he had to explain to *someone* what had happened to him growing up and growing old.

But how to do that? His deliverance came in the resolution that the explanation of Steven Ribman would reside in a book, a place where people could find him after he was gone. He had toyed with the idea after his father died, but the idea died as well.

Now his project began in earnest. On a day a week ago, in this month of August, the day his decision became rock solid and his vision of a bound volume bearing his name became crystal clear, he had seated himself at the computer in the den, opened a blank page in the word processor, and boldly began typing an introduction and a few sentences of the first chapter. That was all he wrote in seven days, but at least it was a start.

He had not revealed to his wife, Evelyn, why he was spending so much time lately at the computer. She hadn't asked. Maybe she hadn't noticed. Maybe he should leave it at that. Writing a book? That might get a laugh out of her. He could treat it as simply a private pastime. Why bother to mention it?

However, the effort would tie up too much of his life. He will *have* to tell her.

Standing painfully on his toes, he stretched upward and peered at a shelf above. Little round cookie tins decorated with multicolored birds sat next to an empty crystal whiskey decanter with a chip on the stopper. Family treasures. His hand touched a small, glossy plastic container and pulled it forward. A label read *My Gift for You.* He removed the cover. Inside was the umber, imitation-leather-bound journal he had given his son, Robert, for his eighteenth birthday. His thumb opened the book to the first page where Robert had started to write in his usual, very slanted characters: "Wednesday, May 25, 1977—This will be a record of my journey to my dream job and to untold excitement." The line of pencil marks trailed off into a few indecipherable words. The rest of the page and all the other pages were blank.

A lot had happened to Robert since his high school graduation, but those moments of joy and those descents into despair had never been logged in. A disappointment for Steve, the gift was never used. But he was no one to judge. *His* past was not posted anywhere either. Soon that would change.

He would write a book, his gift to Robert, a book with all the tall tales that he had planned to tell his son when the two of them sat down to share some coffee, or maybe two mugs of beer.

But those opportunities never came. Robert grew up, got married, and moved away. He seldom dropped by any more, and when he did, he never stopped long enough to relate how his wife, Joan, was doing or how things were going on his job at the insurance company. He would let himself in the front door, wave to Steve, possibly add a "Hi, dad," and run to Evelyn to ask her a question about something—like drapery. There were many things he wanted to tell Robert, but his tall offspring never stopped walking through the house long enough. Robert's presence was more like an apparition.

Where was the box? One carton looked promising. He reached in and pulled out a worn, corroded light switch. He knew there were nine more, exactly the same, mixed in with strands of wire, odd connectors, and ugly outlet plates that will never get used.

When they bought the house, Evelyn had asked him to replace the cheap, noisy toggles with illuminated silent switches. How many decades ago was that? The switch in his hand belonged in some exhibition of ancient artifacts; they will probably bury him with one.

Working in these close quarters, between overloaded storage racks and Evelyn's car, was an exhausting chore, his sixty-eight years adding to the effort. He took a deep breath, a mistake. The small billow of smoky, microscopic dirt particles unearthed when he tugged the boxes, swirled inside his nose, clinging and biting. With a nervous movement, his hand pushed back the gray hair from his forehead. If only he could see what he was doing. He looked up, despairingly, at the shadowy ceiling where he had planned, but failed, to install another overhead light.

A year ago, he had worked up the determination, along with a promise to Evelyn, to do a thorough job of discarding all the useless relics that had been long-banished to the garage—and Evelyn could vouch that he had made a heroic attempt. But replacing the leaking water heater took precedence. Oh, yes, and then came the roof repairs, along with the week-long debate over whether to refinish it with rock or tile. When those crises had passed, he reassured Evelyn all the junk would go.

But now little fragments of sentiment weakened that promise as he looked at the ancient piece of memorabilia, the light switch, turning it in his hand, flicking the actuator. Maybe it will come in handy some day. Sure. He tossed it back in the box.

As he peered into the better illuminated shelves, new clutter came into view. At the rear of one shelf in a rusty tray were the little disc-shaped wire brushes that fit on a drill—used once. They were also on the to-go list. Now they were exhibit A of the thoughtfulness of his wife, a busy housekeeper who drove ten miles to find them for his birthday. She was so pleased when he unwrapped and opened the metal box with a loud cheer, her face beaming with incredible excitement. That birthday, that precious moment, was too important to forget. It should have been recorded in a document somewhere, but he kept no diary. Maybe he should start one now—before his brain dried up completely. The wire brushes could stay a little longer.

He leaned back against Evelyn's car emplaced solidly and silently behind him. Its bulk was difficult to work around—too easy to scratch—yet too much trouble to back out into the driveway. He looked down at the back of his hands and along his arms for possible scrapes where the skin, now growing paper thin, bled at the touch of any sharp edge.

The fatigue was making him careless; objects were catching on his sleeve and falling on the floor. Perhaps this search should be postponed until the morning when the sun sends strong light into the crevices between all the junk.

It was apparent to him now that the paraphernalia that crowded the shelves were more than tools and souvenirs. He was surrounded by objects that were players in a long string of events that represented the existence of S. Ribman. They will all be here, on display, when he was gone.

Adding to his sadness was the realization that they will mean nothing to Robert who will inherit the task of disposing of them, who, someday, will pick up a brittle, black extension cord, smile slightly, and toss it in the trash. *These artifacts are a record of my life, Robbie.* Behind each dusty box and puzzling curio is a story worth telling, enough stories to fill several volumes.

On the shelf nearest the floor was a row of three battered, bottled water boxes. As he pushed them apart, the lettering on the side of one became visible. Printed with a blunt, black marking pen in Ev's lettering was the word PAPER. That should be it. He pulled it toward the edge of the shelf and flipped the lid open. Inside was the bundle of red, green, and gold Christmas wrappings that Evelyn said she couldn't part with. *Wrong box.*

From behind him came the familiar squeak of the hinges of the door leading to the kitchen. He looked up to see Evelyn, her arm outstretched, holding the door wide-open. "Steve, what are you looking for?"

He closed the lid on the box of wrappings, shoved it back against the wall, and looked up at her. "My printer is out of paper. I was sure there were a couple of reams here somewhere."

"Dinner is almost ready."

He stood erect, surveying the pyramid of boxes at his feet. "Can you hold off for a while? I've got a project going on the computer. I've got one lousy page to print. I'm out of paper and I don't want to run to the store if I don't have to."

"How much time do you need?"

"Give me fifteen minutes."

He watched her turn to leave, then stop to look back at him. Her voice was very melodious. "It's your favorite—pot roast." She was always the considerate wife; now the guilt set in.

"Okay, give me ten minutes."

Evelyn again started to step away, but paused. "I might be the guilty party. I think I put your box of paper in that old cupboard to your right. Don't you want a flashlight?"

He reached over to a large peg board on the wall. "I have one here." With a touch, a small, black, cylindrical object dropped into his hand. His thumb depressed a rubbery bump on the side, and a white beam danced over the surroundings.

Evelyn moved back into the kitchen, snapping the door shut. Obeying her suggestion, Steve stepped sideways to reach the aging wooden cupboard bought at a garage sale for five dollars, the one with the faded grey paint job and a door latch that needed replacement. When was the last time he looked inside? He pulled on the door; it opened, creaking sharply. The ray from his flashlight illuminated a large, blue and white carton with the label MULTIPURPOSE COPY PAPER. He sighed.

He started to lift the carton; it was heavy. A sharp pain crossed his chest. He froze, holding the carton motionless for an instant, then lowering it slowly to the cement floor. He remained slightly bent, bracing himself on the cupboard shelf. The chest pains were not a surprise; they came, they went, but each time they were terrifying. Maybe it's his heart; maybe it isn't. His father had worn a pacemaker; his heart stopped anyway. Steve pushed on his breastbone with his fingers. It was probably just a muscle cramp. That's all. He bent again, opened the blue and white box, and retrieved a ream of paper which he placed it on the hood of the car.

The small, gleaming digital clock on the wall came into focus. The thought about his father, the numbers glowing in the dark, took him back in time. It was an evening like this, eight years past, that his sister, Alice, called to tell him their father, Arthur, had died from heart failure.

He had listened to her on the handset in the garage. "It was about thirty minutes ago," she said. "It was bad, Steve." Her voice was soft and unsteady. "He had phoned me about an hour before and asked me to stop by; he said he was feeling punk. A short time later his friend, Ed, phoned me; he was visiting dad when it happened—when the attack came on. Ed had already called the emergency team. I arrived right after the ambulance got there."

The words Alice spoke, the emotions they aroused in him were returning. He remembered the evening well, standing with the phone pressed hard against his ear, overcome with numbness, not really hearing what Alice had said after "Dad has died," barely seeing the digital clock and the gray-blue garage wall in front of him, the same wall that was forever a canvas of that memory.

He did remember a few of her words well—too well. "The emergency guys put the defibrillator paddles on dad and shocked him over and over, but he didn't respond." Then Alice hesitated, as if the description was too painful. "They asked me if they should continue. I couldn't stand watching him being jolted like that, Steve. I said no." There was a quiet sob. Her words began breaking up, becoming almost inaudible. "I will always wonder if letting them try once more might have brought him back."

He felt her agony. His voice was restrained, "Dad always taught us to do what we thought was right. You were being a good daughter."

Then she began crying more than talking. "I'll call later about the funeral plans."

The vision of his sister standing, helpless, next to her father's body, watching as the medical team attempted to revive him, was unreal and inerasable. It was not her responsibility to make the call on forcing life back into a human being she loved. And had he been there with her, he could have done no better. He tried to speak, but there was nothing left to say to her. His mind shut down. He must have mumbled some kind of good-bye as he replaced the handset.

The death of his mother, Julianna, two years earlier, was different. Evelyn and Robert waited at home. The rest of the family—Arthur, Alice, and Steve—had sat at the mother's bedside through the night, watching, listening, poised to detect some movement under her blanket, some sound from her pale, still lips, praying for some miracle. They never knew the moment when she left them, but when the morning came, they took her away.

The soreness around his heart subsided. Thank God! It wasn't too bad. The worst occurrence of a chest spasm was that night in bed two years ago when a pain came—out of nowhere—that was excruciating. It burned like fire from his neck down and across his rib cage. He knew that was *it*.

Evelyn drove him to the emergency room at the nearest hospital where they lifted him into a wheel chair, transferred him to a bed in a small, drapery shrouded enclosure, and hooked him up to the electrocardiograph. The young doctor entered, introduced himself, and looked at the paper spilling out of the machine. He said, "There's nothing wrong with your heart. You're having an attack of the devil's gripe, a virus. It's not too common; I heard about it in medical school. It will pass." The young doctor left.

He remembered looking up from the bed at the vital signs monitor above his head. Some numbers were flashing. What did they mean? The *devil's gripe*? What was that? In the medical dictionary he opened a week later at the library, the condition was correctly spelled "Devil's Grippe." Aptly named. The pain had felt as though the devil had his claws deep between his ribs, *gripping* every muscle in his chest. The young doctor had mispronounced it.

He turned his thoughts back to his mission in the garage. The glowing numerals on the digital clock above the tool board were a reminder that ten minutes had passed. Evelyn will be after him. The pain that stretched below his collar bones disappeared, but he became very conscious of the thumping of his heart.

He started to lift the box of copy paper again, then put it aside on the floor, noticing the exposed box beneath, a very worn and dusty carton with some faded lettering on top: DAD'S. He knew what it contained. Alice had sent him that box about a month after the funeral. The brief note she had pasted on the side said, "Steve, these are dad's things." Whatever that meant.

When the box arrived, he had hesitated opening it to look inside. He felt very uncomfortable with the prospects of what might be there; he hadn't accepted his father's death. It didn't seem right going through his father's private possessions. But standing there, touching it, made him reconsider; there might be something inside he was meant to see.

A small knife he kept on the workbench easily cut through the tape at the top; the flaps parted. A folded slip of paper with Alice's handwriting sat on the top, waiting to be read. The note was a brief explanation of the contents with a longer story of Alice's attempts to round up dad's documents. He tossed it back in without fully reading it.

The note landed on a small, very old address book with a scuffed, brown cover that he had seen his father drop in a dresser drawer. He reached to touch it, then briskly pulled his hand back. It was though the older Ribman was standing beside him, watching, asking, "Why are you going through my stuff, Stevie?" Why was he? Nothing pertained to him.

Convinced of that, he had quickly closed and re-sealed the box with cheap paper packing tape, placed it on the shelf where it had remained, out sight for eight years, never given a thought until now.

The adhesive on the tape he had so carefully applied was now dry and brittle. Perhaps another brief look at the contents was in order. With a slight pull of his finger, the packing tape disintegrated, and the lid flaps rose.

At the top of the assortment of mostly paper goods sat the old, brown address book. He picked it up and let it fall open. Inside, on page after page, were the names, phone numbers and addresses of his father's friends from decades past. There was an entry for Ed Godar, his friend who had called for help when the heart attack occurred. The name took him back in time. Near the age of seven he was introduced to Ed who came to the house one evening to visit Arthur and Julianna. Sitting on the piano bench in the living room, holding a drink, Ed reached out and shook his hand. Funny, Ed was the only friend of his dad he had ever met. And now his name came up again. He put the book aside.

Next, a large Kraft envelope came into view which he lifted out. Inside he felt a thin clump of paper that he extracted. There was newsprint on it. He could barely make out the bold letters at the top: AFB CHRONICLE. This rang a bell. Arthur had worked as a lead inspector at the airbase during the second world war. There was a large photograph of a group of people on the front page; the small type of the caption was unreadable in the poor light. He studied the faces; the strong features of a woman caught his eye. He looked closer, but the flashlight flickered off and the image disappeared in the darkness. He slid the paper back in the envelope, stuffing it along the side of the box.

He pointed the defective flashlight downward, sharply knocking it against a shelf ledge in frustration, pressing the button repeatedly, cursing. The light returned, reflecting brightly from a thick, folded document which he removed and opened with a few tugs. It appeared to be an artfully decorated form of some kind, laminated. Dad laminated everything. The printing read "Julia Allenton Elementary School, Certificate of Penmanship awarded to Arthur Ribman on this day of May 12, 1916" At the bottom was the signature of Emmett Clarke, principal.

The image of the certificate struck him like a signal, linking him to the past. He remembered one evening, at the age of fifteen, when his father walked over to him at the kitchen table where he was reading and writing; his father was holding that very piece of decorated paper at his side. He watched Steve's hand as it moved across the page, distilling the plot of a book lying open in front of him. He asked, "Steve, did I ever tell you how good *my* handwriting was?"

"I'm not sure, dad. I have a book report due tomorrow. Can you tell me later?" His father paused, thought a moment, then left, never mentioning the subject again.

Had he injured his father's feelings? Maybe it was not that important to him. An image came: his father as a boy. What, twelve years old? He was standing at the front of a classroom, smiling. The teacher was displaying his certificate. "Arthur has earned this," she likely said. He could see his father reaching up to receive his prize. The image blurred and faded.

He knew his father had a large collection of clippings, books, and business papers that became his biography. Alice's note said most of dad's souvenirs of a lifetime had been thrown away when he knew the end was imminent. She wrote that on one of her last visits to his house, about two weeks before he died, she watched her father, staggering, carry an armload of bags, probably filled with books, letters, obsolete files, that he dropped into the trash bins. Yet he kept *this* award! He kept this faded, wrinkled, cheaply printed form until his death. It meant something to him. He should have let his father brag about his penmanship. *What a prig I was!*

He folded the certificate and returned it to the box, beginning now to wonder if there was anything else in there to inspect that could reveal some interest or achievement of the Ribman senior Steve had never bothered to ask about.

There was a door click. He turned toward Evelyn's thin silhouette blocking the warm light of the kitchen. She chirped, "Hey, handsome, your ten minutes were up a while ago."

"Yeah," he grunted. "I found what I was looking for." She backed away and closed the door.

Steve let the stiff document fall back into the box. He folded the flaps and shoved it against the wall. But the damage was done; more incidents were coming to life: memories began to surface—his father fixing the old Buick—memories that had disappeared. To remind himself this was today, not then, he looked at the calendar hanging over the washing machine, a page displaying the Grand Canyon, overprinted with 1997 in bold numerals. The month was September. His focus moved down to the space labeled Friday, the seventh—this day—the day that he actually made the effort to continue writing his book. He grabbed the ream of paper he had placed on the car hood and cradled it under his arm.

His objective achieved, he opened the kitchen door, thumbed the light switch off, and joined Evelyn in the family room.

At the dinner table, Evelyn placed before him a plate with a mound of the pot roast.

"I made spaetzle to go with that; want some?"

"Sure." He unfolded a napkin.

From a steaming bowl she spooned a scoop of tiny, doughy lumps onto his dish. She set the bowl aside and tapped the table in front of him.

"I have a hair appointment tomorrow. I might have it cut shorter around the sides and back. What do you think?"

He leaned sidewise to inspect, envisioning the absence of the strands that covered her ears and neck. "You mean as short as when I first met you. Didn't you have bangs then?"

She threw her head back, laughing. "I never had bangs. You must be thinking of some other woman." She laughed again.

He smiled to go along with the humor she found in his remark. Okay, maybe she never had bangs. He peered at her, accepting that time had brought changes to her features. Her face now was not that of the woman he met and married, but the little curves and lines around her mouth and eyes that made her stand out in a crowd were still there. Her hair was forever the shock of gold, helped along with a little coloring. She had let her eyebrows grow back to normal width. Behind slender, silver-framed spectacles her brown eyes always looked upon him favorably.

She patted her temple. "Don't worry. You'll like the new me."

His mind was still on the box in garage and its contents, but Evelyn was in the mood to talk.

"What's this project you're working on?" she asked.

"I'm trying to write a book." As he spoke, he knew she would ask more questions he could not answer.

"You never told me you wanted to write a book."

He did not. It would not have led to a pleasant, productive discussion for him to describe his awakening that day, the day he took a long look at his reflection in the bathroom mirror, a reminder of his own mortality. And he certainly, certainly could never, ever mention the jabs in his chest.

"In fact," she complained, "I didn't know you had an urge to write *anything*."

He admitted, "I know; I never told you this story. In high school, one of my English teachers, a young guy, was fired up on the beauties of literary expression. He introduced us to a piece he loved. He recited it for us, line by line, explaining the interpretation as he went. I still remember the first sentence: *Awake! For morning in the bowl of night has flung the stone that puts the stars to flight.* Somehow he stirred something up inside me."

"That's from some novel?"

"No, it's a poem. As I listened to the instructor say the words, make us aware of the meanings, the imagery, I began thinking: I want to become an author, to write stuff like that myself."

"Why didn't you."

"My mother discouraged me. She saw me ending up as a starving 'pencil-pusher.' Both my mother and father ganged up on me and convinced me to plan on a more practical profession."

Evelyn's arms went up in a show of admiration. "And you did, Steve. You've had a great career. Look around. We've raised a son, own a beautiful home, nicely furnished—my ideas, of course." She winked.

"So how long have you been toying with this book notion?"

He knew she was just being conversational, but she deserved an answer. "When the idea came to me years ago, I considered it foolish. So, I never mentioned it; other things came up, as they always do; I let go of the book. But now—now, I've got a little time." He hoped that served as a reason.

"Well, what happened that changed your mind?"

She was digging deeper; that was her nature. He raised a forkful of vegetables to his lips. "You know I've never done any writing—other than the reports at the office. Those weren't fiction—although some people might label them that." He grinned, snorted, and began choking on a piece of potato he had not swallowed. "Something came over me. I mean this seriously, Ev. I'm getting old. There are some thoughts I carry around, thoughts I want to leave on paper."

Evelyn put her fork down and stroked his arm. "At your age do you think you can find the energy?" She placed her index finger on her forehead. "Can you reprogram that tired, old brain to start thinking like an author?"

"Well, I had some doubts at first, but then I've had doubts about everything I ever accomplished in life."

Smiling, eyes opened wide, she tapped her fork on her plate. "That sounds like a creative way to spend some of your free time; you were complaining you have nothing to do."

He wanted very much to believe her, but she was just being kind; she was humoring him. Even as she encouraged his literary endeavors, she was probably dismayed over the household projects canceled for the lack of a handyman.

He watched her cut the small chunks of beef on her plate into even tinier pieces. The conversation on writing a book, digging up the past, didn't trigger any response from her. In all their years together, she had never mentioned any recurring memories of her own. Maybe one or two childhood incidents now and then: the neighbor's cat that scratched her arm severely, leaving the awful streaks of her blood on her wrist. There must have been *some* times in her young life when her wishes came true that she will forever recall. And there had to be those days when fate snatched away a piece of her existence, a possession lost, a pet that died, leaving her to face a reality too brutal to accept.

Next to Evelyn's plate was a pile of mail delivered that day that she began sorting. They continued to eat without speaking. Steve wondered if she understood his need to capture his life, or did she accept it as another passing craze, like his foolish spurt of volunteer work for the city.

He snatched a breadstick from the stack on the table and rolled it slowly in his fingers, using the time to phrase his confession. "I had big plans for my retirement, but they didn't pan out. I don't have the energy anymore. Actually, it was easier to go back and work half-days." He saw her questioning look; he assured her, "I'll still have time to do some writing."

Evelyn began picking up the plates on the table. "What's the book about?"

"It will be about my life."

"You mean an autobiography?"

She walked to the sink and dropped the dishes in with a clatter. Steve turned in his chair to face her. "No. I'm considering a story about a man who reflects on the events of his past."

"Like a memoir? They're very popular."

"No, it will be a novel—the main character is an older guy—someone like me. But it will be written in the third person."

She walked back to face him, wiping her hands with a towel. Her eyebrows went up as she asked, "Do you have a plot?

"That's what I'm working on."

She nodded as if she thoroughly understood the totality of his struggle, but he sensed she had a dozen more questions.

Working on a plot? There wasn't a hint of a plot. But she needed an answer. What could he tell her? He envisioned the words printed in crisp, black letters on the inside flap of the book's glossy dust cover. He sat back, looked at the ceiling and recited slowly for her benefit, inventing words as he spoke.

"This is the story of a man who wonders if he has passed over some opportunities in life and could have been a better person." He hesitated, gesturing toward the ceiling at an imaginary line of type. "Little bits and pieces from his past begin to show up to haunt him."

She watched his act then held out her palm. "Give me an example."

"What?" His mind was still focused on the glossy dust cover. "Example of what?"

"Bits from the past that haunt your guy."

Steve paused. Should he open the safe of his mind? In all the years they were married he had never told Evelyn much about his childhood, except, perhaps, trivial incidents, like catching the mumps. The pain, and sometimes happiness, of those other events were beyond description in casual conversation.

She pulled out a chair from the table, sat down, displaying interest in his answer.

One incident came to his mind, but it wouldn't be easy explaining. "When I was about ten years old, I challenged my best friend, Ralph, to a foot race down the alley. He took me up on it and I finished way ahead. He finally caught up with me, breathing hard. I'm not sure how he felt. He was smiling; I was feeling superior. But I shouldn't have done that. It's one of those things that's been bothering me."

"Why?"

"He was not a strong kid; he was diabetic. I remember watching his mother give him an insulin shot."

"Maybe he never thought of himself as handicapped. Maybe just being able to race with you was more important than winning."

The image was becoming too vivid: a small boy running behind him, pounding the hard pavement of the long alley, thin legs churning, lungs working hard for breath, unable to keep up. "I've always known what I did was cruel." His hand went up to cover his eyes. His head trembled. "I have this nightmare of a memory of him plodding after me, struggling to keep up."

Evelyn asked, "Have you ever thought about visiting him on some excuse? You know; you could start chatting about the old days; tell him how wrong you were to outrun him."

He began shifting in his chair, his arm reaching up and rubbing the back of his neck for no reason. "He died when he was twenty-six."

She squinted in disapproval. "That story is kind of dismal. I wouldn't put that one in the book." She straightened herself in her chair, her face relaxed. "What else does your main character think about?"

Suddenly he became aware of the enormity of his project. Here, sitting at the empty dinner table, hands clasped and resting on his lap, facing Evelyn, the whole evening ahead did not contain minutes enough to relate what else his main character thought about. He would give her a cogent summary.

"Well, he comes to the realization that he never spent enough time talking to his father, whom he loved very much."

Evelyn reacted, eyebrows raised, as though he were confessing some long-hidden personal revelation. "Were you thinking about *your* father?"

"Sure."

He could tell her about the penmanship award. He should tell a lot of people. Dad would have wanted him to. But she might want him to drag out the box and show her the wrinkled document. *Better pass on that.* There were other stories he could relate.

He pressed his fingers on the tabletop, spread as if reaching ten ivory-sheathed keys, his head bent as if listening to some rich but soundless chord. "My father loved to play the piano. We had an old, upright in our house, the only one he could raise enough money for. Often, he accompanied himself singing *I'm always chasing rainbows*. That was one of the first songs I learned from him as a kid."

The remark brought Evelyn's head and hand up. "Is that the song I hear you humming around the house?"

"Probably. He taught me the words to a lot of other songs he learned as a young man living in Texas, songs you've never heard."

Evelyn began tapping her fingers on the table, mimicking Steve. "I'm surprised you never learned to play an instrument—to play some of those songs."

"He wanted me to learn to play piano; he wanted that very much. He signed me up for private lessons; something he really couldn't afford, Ev. I wasn't too interested and wanted to quit, so I told the instructor my dad didn't have the money. It was funny; I was doing so well the teacher offered to continue the lessons without charge."

"Then you *did* learn how to play. You never told me."

He wondered if she could detect the emotion building up in him. "I didn't take the offer. I guess I was interested in other kid stuff—stupid. I disappointed my father—as usual; that is one of my many regrets."

She pursed her lips. "You've just told me two sad memories. That doesn't sound like much of a plot. Where does the tension come in?"

He looked down at the weave of the white cloth on the table, silent. His life didn't have a plot. But it had some significance. Wasn't that enough?

Evelyn tossed her hands in small circles. "Doesn't there have to be some . . . problem? . . . something that needs a resolution?" She tilted her head to look up into his eyes.

"I don't see it as that kind of a book," he said. "Haven't figured out how to put it all together. Maybe there are some good examples out there. Can you suggest any?"

"Why are you asking me?"

"You read a lot. You're in that book club."

"That's right," she admitted. "But the books our club members put on the suggested reading list usually involve notorious affairs of proper people or heavy family drama; nothing like you're talking about. You should have read more yourself."

"I never had the time."

She waved at a stack of newspapers on the chair at her side. "I saw an article the other day that said several thousand new book titles get published each year. Do you think very many people will want to buy your book?

"It doesn't matter. I have to write it."

"You *have* to?"

"I want to leave something behind, something that tells people about me." He took a breath and tightened his jaw. "Something more than a headstone."

Evelyn raised her shoulders a bit and moved her attention to the pile of mail, accepting his words in a quiet manner.

He hoped he had convinced her he was serious. Even if fate never allowed him to finish, he had to start putting words down. God willing, there was still time. If he was careful, the pain in his chest might not come again for months. His hand pressed his shirt front.

"Why are you rubbing your chest?" she asked.

"Was I?"

Evelyn tried another topic. "I've read that completing a novel is a long, stressful journey. I had a history teacher in high school tell us he was writing a book based on his ancestors. He said working through it was like giving birth to a baby— as if he'd know."

As she observed his face for his reaction, she picked up a bit of a cookie from a bowl on the table and placed it into her mouth, chewing slowly.

He watched her eyes. *She needs a minute to decide how to politely express the doubts she is entertaining about my ever making a book happen.* She was only trying to save him from future disappointment. She probably envisioned him spending late hours at the computer, struggling to salvage some amateurish narrative, trying to act the good soldier when the rejection letters arrived.

He asked, "You think I'll be wasting my time?"

"No. Everybody should have something they love to do. If writing a book is one of the things on your list, then you should pursue that."

"I can't put it off any longer."

The tone of her voice grew firm. "I'll say it again: it will take a lot of energy and persistence, Steve. And a *lot* of material. Are you ready with all that?"

Material? There was an ample supply: facing sharp-tongued school teachers, pondering the death of friends, the exhausting job searches and interviews, discovering Evelyn at the office, listening to his father play the piano. "The stuff is all there." He assured her, "The book will write itself."

Her face had doubt written all over it. "I know you have some very interesting stories, and some sad ones, but how can you be sure about the details? You never kept a journal—or did you?"

"Nope. Never kept a journal." He slid back in his chair and tapped the table. "I do have some letters I wrote to my mother, letters I wrote when I was in the Navy. She saved them and gave them back to me when she got old. There's a lot of history there."

Evelyn grinned. "Well, you have *me* you know. I can remind you of some of your escapades. Just ask me."

"I may do that."

"Why don't you include that visit to my sister, Valerie? Remember? You showed their little boy, Danny, that sleight-of-hand trick with the penny. Then you gave him the coin to keep. Remember how thrilled he was? He kept saying, 'Magic penny. magic penny.' You made him very happy."

Her sister's house? When was that? He found himself listening, but there was no image. Her words described a staged event, a movie he had never seen. Then the realization took hold again. There were elements of his life, like this one, that had disappeared: faces, voices, romps, scrapes, lost pieces as important as those he *could* remember. It would indeed be a challenge describing a life when not all of the important incidents were there to inspect at will.

A terrible unease fell over him. If he were honest, he should say to her, "Evelyn, something's happening to my mind. I'm frightened. I can't remember things I should know." But why frighten her? He had to accept that he was capable of forgetting—all the more reason to get started on the book.

Evelyn waited for his reaction to her replay of his magical performance at her sister's house. Stalling, groping for a response, he patted her hand to show his appreciation. A pretense of remembering might be wise at this moment. "Your help is important, dear," he said. I'll think about where that story might fit in my book."

First, she smiled at his acceptance of her contribution, then frowned. "Who can you get to publish it?"

"I have no idea."

Her question triggered an item on his mental to-do list. He plucked a newspaper clipping from the breast pocket of his shirt and laid it in front of her. "It's a class on book writing."

She looked down at a small display ad. She leaned forward to read the fine print aloud. "Best-Seller Basic Training. A beginner's workshop on novel writing and publishing."

"It runs for six Saturdays," he explained. "The first class is tomorrow morning. I've signed up."

"Where do you have to go?"

"It's there in the ad. It's sponsored by Garlandale Community College; they have an off-campus classroom in the All Traders shopping mall. Not far."

"*Six* weeks?" Evelyn exclaimed, emphasizing the *six* as though she hadn't heard it right the first time. "I guess you'll be covering a lot of subject matter on how novels are written. It looks like your book is going to take a while."

Yes, it *will* take a while, but he was sure the workshop will be the means for him to honor his commitment to the book; everything will get set down on paper. The little twinges in the chest were there to remind him he didn't have a lot of time.

He slid his chair back, rose, and started down the hallway.

Evelyn looked up. "Where are you headed? Did you want some dessert?"

"I'll pass on the dessert. I'll be in the den. I have to print and fill out the application form for the workshop tomorrow." As he paced slowly away, he thought again about the question on the form that asks why he wanted to take the workshop. Maybe he will use the same answer he gave Evelyn.

STORY TWO

DR. DOHLSTRAM

WRITTEN across the top of the whiteboard in the front of the classroom were the words BEST-SELLER BASIC TRAINING. A young woman sitting at Steve's table raised her hand to get the attention of the instructor, a very mature woman with short, steel colored hair, wearing loose, dark pants, a gray blouse, and an even darker gray blazer. Her eyeglasses dangled from a neck cord.

The young woman asked, "Mrs. McFarland, before we break, can you answer a question about the best book size to choose?" The instructor waved away the question. "In next week's session we will cover trim sizes. I'll go into the factors—like applicability to the subject matter, the genre, book length, marketability—all that." Mrs. McFarland turned away and began erasing the whiteboard she had covered with publishing terminology.

Steve closed his notebook, slid his pen into his breast pocket, and looked at the men and women converging on the door that led to the mall. *Aspiring authors.* They obviously didn't know any more about writing a best-seller than he did or they wouldn't be in the class. The question lingering in his mind hadn't been answered. He wasn't sure *what* the question was. How should his book come together? He rose and glanced over the empty chairs, nodding to Mrs. McFarland as he left the room.

On the sidewalk of the tree-lined mall he leaned against a light-post, mulling over his choices of returning home or sitting on one of the dusty benches the merchants provided, a refuge where he could phrase those questions in his notebook that he failed to ask Mrs. McFarland.

Every one of the shoppers was walking briskly, as if urged on by a mission. He lacked one. The breeze was growing stronger, tugging at his jacket. Stay or go? If he drove back to the house, Evelyn would want a minute-by-minute recounting of the class topics. If she asked enough questions, she would discover he had acquired some interesting facts about book marketing, but nothing to lead him out of the maze he was in. She might suggest he drop the class, putting him on the defensive; he wanted to stay with the workshop. A few minutes more spent gathering his ideas wouldn't matter.

Looking down the walkway he made out the words "The Select Cup" jutting from the rough, gray stucco façade on one of the shoulder-to-shoulder store fronts. That must be the new coffee bar he had heard about, probably a better sanctuary for composing thoughts then a busy sidewalk. This was a good time to check it out.

He walked quickly to the entrance and paused a moment for three young women, exiting, laughing, juggling large paper cups as they breezed past him. Once inside the doorway of the coffee shop, Steve scrutinized the layout for a place to sit. The room was amply furnished with tall, three-foot wide, round tables, each flanked by two or three chairs—tall, stool-like, with back rests—all occupied. There was a counter with a line of bench seats along the windows, but they were all filled as well. He made note of a single empty table in the far corner.

There was a sense of energy in the room, a buzz of voices, undiscernible conversations, and a swarm of customers. The early afternoon light from the large windows along one wall fell on other people like him seeking a retreat from the harsh demands of the day, some reading newspapers, some twisting paper cups in solitude, some in deep discussion with others at their table.

The service counter was straight ahead. A male cashier wearing a wrinkled, white, paper garrison cap noticed his approach and smiled at him. Steve stepped forward, looking up at the ornately framed menu. The smiling young man asked, "What can I get for you, Sir?".

Steve pulled a five-dollar bill from his wallet and dropped it on the counter. "Give me a medium-sized cup of your strongest stuff."

His order and change were set down before him. Holding the steaming liquid in one hand and his notebook in the other, he turned into the large room, comforted by the smell of coffee. Now feeling unusually creative, he could sit quietly at a table, sip the warm liquid, and make a record of the ideas that had come to him in class.

He stopped short. The distant, lone, empty table he had chosen for his use had been taken by two men wearing tan shirts, dark neckties, and badges. Closer was another table with two chairs and a single individual leaning on an elbow, an older man holding his cup at the bottom, staring toward the wall of windows. The hair on his head was sparse; a brief, distinctive, silver-gray beard graced his chin, very recognizable. Steve remembered seeing him near the rear of the classroom.

He wove his way through the tight maze of tables and people. Ahead was a group of energetic college students, some waving their arms dangerously close to his cup. He avoided them. He whispered "pardon me" three times as he carefully and painfully maneuvered around a very aged, almost motionless, woman in a grim black wheelchair blocking his path to the empty seat, a chair with light blue wheels and a contrasting bright fabric back: pink poppies on a gray field. Her back was toward him, but he could see the woman's gnarled hands at her waist. She leaned forward as if listening to the chatter surrounding her.

He stood before the table, looked directly at the solitary male customer, and spoke. "Mind if I join you?"

The man looked up and grinned. "Sure, make yourself at home. Don't we know each other?"

"Yeah, classmates." Steve laid his notebook and coffee cup on the table, pulled out a chair, and lifted himself onto the seat. He offered his hand. "I'm Steve Ribman."

The man was holding an impressive rust-colored portfolio which he snapped closed. He reached over to Steve and completed a firm handshake. "I'm Richard Dohlstram. If you want to be formal, it's Doctor Richard Dohlstram. But I'm not a medical doctor." He leaned back and raised his coffee cup in a toast. "May this road lead to prominent authorship." In turn, bowing his head slightly, Steve lifted his cup. "Here's to success with our novels."

A look of amusement lit Richard's face. "Well, my book won't be a novel. It will be more like a lengthy research report. I stated that on the questionnaire we filled out on course objectives. Our instructor, Mrs. McFarland, warned me that most of the class work involves fiction, but I told her that if she can put up with my questions, I will take serious notes in case I wanted to write another *Arrowsmith*. My book will be about sleep disorders."

Steve raised his eyebrows. "I don't have any of those, but I may buy your book anyway."

He had a vision of this new friend, looking professional in a white lab jacket, clipboard in hand, bending over a sleeper, taking notes. He asked, "How did you get involved with that? Why did you pick that subject?"

Richard tapped his chest. "You might say the subject picked me. I'm the Director of the Unified Health Resource Center here in town. We provide guidance and programs for company employees. You know—for a healthier workplace environment—and sometimes for health issues in the home. That's our motto."

"Do a lot of people have sleep problems?"

"Yes, a lot. But most go to their family physician. Over the years a few cases came across my desk involving some highly-paid, stressed-out managers who couldn't handle the day from lack of a good night's rest. One dozed off at the wheel and almost killed someone. Their companies *strongly* suggested these executives see me. My book will be about how those guys got that way and how we straightened them out."

Steve turned his head a little sideways, questioning. "But you said you're not an MD."

Richard swirled the coffee in his cup. "That's right. My doctorate is in clinical psychology. What do you do, Steve?"

"I'm with the recreation and park district."

"Hey, an opportunity to relax, have fun, and commune with nature. But then, you probably have your own hectic moments."

"Fortunately, I do have a light schedule. I retired last year from my position as planning director. But they called me back as a consultant, so let's say I'm partially retired. I stop by the office now and then. I've got the time to do some writing."

Richard nodded approvingly. "If I may ask, what's *your* book about?"

Steve wondered why the question hadn't come sooner. "My wife is prodding me for the same information. The approach hasn't jelled yet. It will be about experiences I feel I must describe that are important to me—memories I've never told anyone." He thought a moment about what he had said, then added, "More correctly, memories I've never had the *chance* to tell anyone."

Steve laughed briefly, then abruptly went silent as the very word "memory" brought up an image. He is sitting on his father's lap in the driver's seat of the old Buick. They are on a Sunday afternoon outing; this is his first driving lesson. His father is working the gas, the brake pedals, and the shift stick. Steve is doing the steering as they navigate the narrow, unused rural byways his father picked for the instruction.

The old, abandoned road they are on needs re-paving badly. The car rolls over a wide crack, suffers a jolt that seems to raise it from the ground. He thinks he has damaged the car. His father laughs,

"You don't have hit *all* the holes, Steve." He shakes off the thought.

He glances at Richard, not sure that he has made his point. "I want to share those memories with other people who recognize how those events can leave footprints in your mind. I guess I want readers to experience them through my words."

Richard looked down, listening to Steve's explanation, then looked up with concern. "So, what do you hope to get out of this workshop?"

Steve threw his arms apart, as if in despair. "Something to tie my ideas together. I don't know what to call it." He floundered, groping for the word. "Structure," he mumbled. Wasn't that the key expression? By his hesitation the wise doctor surely must be perceiving he was a babe in the literary woods.

He felt defensive. "Here's the problem; does it make sense? Throughout the pages the main character is constantly reminded of his past. But there has to be more than just brooding, don't you think? There's got to be some other involvement . . . some other . . . challenge. During the whole damn book what else is my guy doing?"

Richard nodded in an understanding way. "Do you know of any other authors using the same theme? Maybe you can find a book with a style you could—and I hate to use the word—steal some ideas from."

Steve considered the suggestion for a minute. Find a book—where? Sure, ask someone at the reference desk at the library to direct him to the shelf with the introspective novels by old men. He could hear the patient, charitable answer. "Sorry, Mr. Ribman, the library is not cataloged that way."

He gestured at Richard. "Well, fortunately, you don't have that problem with *your* book. You said it's just a long report on lousy sleep patterns. So *why did* you sign up for this course?"

Richard finished his coffee and waved his cup at Steve. "I need to know the rules about formatting this kind of a book. It's not intended for mass marketing. And I don't want it to be so dry and so technical that the average person with a sleep problem wouldn't pick it up." Richard smiled and winked. "On the other hand, it might put them to sleep." He pushed the cuff of his jacket up to check his watch. "Hey, Steve, I've got to get going."

Steve looked down at his empty cup, pushed his chair back, and slid off. "Same here." He tapped Richard's sleeve. "I'll ask you the same question. Aren't there some good examples of hardcovers on sleep out there *you* could use?"

Richard shrugged. "Those I've reviewed didn't impress me. I want my book to be readable, but authentic. And I also need some good instruction on little things—like the rules for citing references—and creating an index."

Customers circled around them, filling the floor, coming and going. Richard began to step away from the table, then pulled back. Three young men wearing dark sweatshirts with emblems of an eagle over the word "GARLANDALE" crowded by, laughing. Steve moved quickly aside, avoiding a jolt, as a young man, dressed in dark blue scrubs, pushed the old woman in the wheelchair toward the entrance, the eye-catching chair with the blue wheels and the bright pink poppies.

As they walked to the exit, Steve looked at Richard and said, "Maybe we can share some coffee next Saturday. I'm open to any suggestions you have about how I might put my novel together. You could suggest an angle that would make it interesting to you."

"I'll have to give that some thought," Richard said as he moved away, tilted his head, and pointed his thumb over his shoulder. "Gotta run." He turned and continued out of the shop.

Steve stepped aside from the customer traffic, raised the cover of his notebook, and looked down at his notes: little hints dropped by Mrs. McFarland to get his writing in motion. There was no glimmer there of a plan for laying everything out. He closed the cover firmly, tucked the notebook under his arm, and headed for the door, stopping at the pastry case. Evelyn might like a raisin scone. He bought two.

When he arrived home, he found a note on the refrigerator from Evelyn stating she was going to the dry cleaners and later to a dentist appointment. Scrawled along the bottom was a list of jobs for him.

He spent most of the afternoon and early evening changing light bulbs and fixing a drip in the kitchen sink faucet, thinking as he tightened the screw on the faucet handle that he should really be in the den typing. What to type? He didn't know. There had to be a way to deal with the thoughts crying to be documented. He dropped a screwdriver and a wrench into a small toolbox at his feet. He washed his hands in the sink and wiped them with a paper towel. He looked out the kitchen window. The daylight had vanished. The garden lights clicked on in the gathering dusk.

A thumping noise, a car door slamming, interrupted his concentration. Through the doorway to the garage he watched Evelyn, holding a large white plastic bag, close the rear hatch of her vehicle. She looked up at him and said, "I got some Chinese take-out for our meal tonight. You good for that?"

He gave her a thumbs up and retreated down the hallway to the den. He switched on the fluorescent desk lamp, slid into the office chair and flipped open the worn notebook on the desk, running his finger down sentences he had underlined. There was nothing there he could convert into a meaningful line of narrative. There was a note recalling his adventuresome assignment by his fourth-grade teacher to get ink from the superintendent in the school basement, a place he didn't even know existed. So what? How will that fit in anywhere?

This was a waste of time. He was drained of all energy, all impulse to write. The fountain of words he expected had dried up. He sat back in the chair and stared at the wall where plaques with his degree and certifications were hung. Those were put there a long time ago, he almost couldn't remember receiving them. On the desk he noticed a pile of envelopes, bills to pay, that Evelyn had dropped off. Those were sufficient excuse to put aside the notebook and any thoughts about penning memorable prose. He will stay busy writing checks until Evelyn summoned him to the table.

Dinner ended. Steve and Evelyn ate the scones with some chamomile tea. She looked at him, searchingly. "How did the class go?"

"I learned a lot of rules." He frowned. "The material we covered today didn't get to the wrinkle

I'm looking for. But I met an interesting fellow at the coffee shop nearby. He's in the class with me."

"He's writing a novel?"

"No, he's into health services. He's putting together a reference on sleep problems."

"So, then, there's no competition as to whose book will be the best."

Steve sighed. "True, but then I don't expect to glean any creative ideas from him either."

Evelyn began gathering up the silverware and plates. "Are you planning to do some writing now? It's getting late. Aren't you tired?"

His voice became spirited. "A little. The woman who is running the workshop said the first rule is to write a little every day. She said some people have more energy in the morning but more creative ideas at night. I don't have either at the moment."

"Well, you sound more motivated than you did yesterday. Why don't you try to write something— now!"

He reached for the teacups. "I will after I help you clear the table."

Evelyn placed her hands on his shoulders and pushed him into the hallway. "Go!"

He walked a few steps toward the den, paused, and looked back. "That's it, Evy, I'm going to dedicate my book to you."

He went into the den, pulled back the chair, and sat down. He needed a little stimulus to write; maybe more than a little. He knew where that could be found. To his right, between the bronze bookends, next to the dictionary was a legal-size envelope. He plucked it out, raised the flap and removed a single, folded sheet of paper, a letter to Robert. He opened it to read what he had composed on the computer a week before.

Robert, I have begun writing a book about my life. I pray that I may be allowed to finish it. It is meant for you to read. If I am fortunate, others may want to read it also, but it is my gift to you.

We have done much for each other and there is no doubt whatsoever about your devotion for me. I believe you would agree I have taken good care of you and respected you as a person. But, Robert, I am distressed by our not grasping the opportunities for us to sit together to talk, for me to answer questions you might have had about the sometimes sad and sometimes funny things that happened to me as I made my way through this world.

Those things I can still remember, those things I never told you, those things that are important for you to know are in my book. With God's grace I will finish it.

Love,
Your Dad

He folded the letter and slid it back into the envelope. The handwriting on the face of the envelope read "To Robert when I am gone."

With a press of a button the computer began to whir. He fell back in the chair to watch the monitor start to glow. Now was the time he needed someone to talk to—someone like his father. Funny, his father never wrote a word in his life, except for some family correspondence, but were his father there, sitting in the other chair watching, hearing, he would, as always, have advice on what to do. That's what Arthur Ribman was good at: listening, not judging, accepting without too much complaint what life gave and took away.

He rested his fingers on the keyboard. Where to start? The memories were bundled neatly into the phases of his growing up, like his pre-teen years, the afternoons with his friends. But that wasn't a safe place to look; it was a place with outcomes sometimes too painful to think about, let alone admit—even to Evelyn. He wished he could erase them, but only death could do that. There were so many ways he went wrong. There was no intention of getting away with mischief; he was just plain stupid, but his behavior must have disappointed his dad sometimes.

There was that terrible summer afternoon. He was playing tag with Ralph and Herbie among the vehicles lining the curb of their street. Laughing and careless, he darted out between two parked cars into the traffic to face an oncoming car that pulled to a screeching halt in front of him. In a state of horror, he recognized the chromium grill poised inches from his body: the front of his father's Buick. There was pounding in his chest, pressure in his cheeks. He looked up at the firm face of his father behind the windshield. It held no expression, but their eyes met. He waved weakly and trotted away.

He expected a long lecture that evening, but never a word was said, a quality he loved in his dad. Arthur Ribman knew that Steven Ribman had been taught a lesson that day in how easy it is to end his existence, a lesson he would remember all his life; and he was right.

That recollection was always there, waiting. But he was troubled by the loss of memories of vast passages of time in his growing up. Most of the faces of teachers and friends in the elementary, high school, and college classes had disappeared, but dozens of images remained for some reason, playing across his mind. There he was in his eighth-grade class, only days before graduation, listening to Mrs. Grantvedt, the Principal, praise them for their efforts and advise them to consider this occasion to be merely a stepping stone to the achievements that lay ahead. Why did he remember that out of all the days at that school? How was he able to remember her long name?

There he was in his senior year at college, writing answers to the questions on Economics in the little blue test book; some of the answers weren't coming. A passing grade in this course was crucial. How sharp that memory! He could even relive the feel of the hard chair as he sat there, his pencil hovering above the empty page, overcome with fear, and, yes, anger. The instructor had never made clear the material to be covered in the final. This was one of the more painful memories that, perhaps, should be left out.

No, he wanted them *all* in the book; but they were a disconnected jumble. How do other authors deal with this dilemma? If only he had someone to sit down with, someone he could toss a few ideas to. Maybe the very astute Dr. Dohlstram could be of help. Even though the good doctor begged off making any suggestions, he might yet if pressed enough. He could snag him again at the coffee shop.

He began to type a word at the top of the blank page staring back at him from the computer monitor. His fingers slid across the keyboard and the letters didn't make sense. He highlighted the letters and hit "Delete."

This wasn't going to be easy. Where to begin? An outline would have helped, but there were too many missing pieces to make one. That subject came up early in the workshop and ended in a debate. One student, the young guy with the long sideburns, argued persuasively that an outline is too restrictive; you go where your characters' motivations take you. But then the very young woman with the burgundy-framed glasses pointed out that an outline gave you a sense of completeness; you could jump ahead and produce chapters that took on more significance, that were crying to be let out.

There were too many options here to deal with. He had to stop juggling them and get down to business. What was on his mind at the *moment*? He would go with that. If he could just summarize it. He wrote to himself, "I must bring myself to cherish this moment while it is here as much as I cherish those moments I failed to live in the past and am now struggling to preserve." He looked at the sentence a long time. Was that really what he meant? That was the problem with every sentence he put up. There were always other tempting ways to express an idea. The thought probably wasn't worth the effort. He deleted the sentence.

Maybe one of the rules Mrs. McFarland wrote on the whiteboard offered a good starting point. He looked to his right at the desk cluttered with two day's mail. He reached across and pulled his notebook out from under a newspaper, opened it and ran his finger down the notes from the class. Yes, here was step one: "Establish a thematic premise for the novel." He didn't have a premise, but now he knew he was lacking something and he knew what to call it. He sat very still for a whole minute then began typing again, speaking the words as they spread across the page, "Premise: elderly man learns late in life the importance of living every moment fully." He was pleased with his grasp of the project. He smiled.

A feeling of optimism began to wipe away the uncertainty dogging him. He had a plan in place. Review the events of his life from the very beginning and document them *now, here*, in plain language. What was his earliest memory? He had surely spent more time with his mother, Julianna, but most of the images he summoned were of his father, coaxing him to do something.

What about his toys? He couldn't believe the beauty of the American Flyer train set, wrapped in glistening paper under the Christmas tree, a set his parents had paid a lot of cash for. In the days that followed, the abundant supply of curved and straight track pieces in the big box enabled him to design elaborate layouts on the living room floor. He had to be careful inserting the pins of one piece of track into the openings of the next piece. Then he snapped the connector to the middle and outside rails of the track. Then he hooked up the red and black wires to the transformer and ran the power cord to the wall.

That was an obscure memory he had almost overlooked. That frightened him. What if his memory was going? Will he be sitting here at the keyboard six months from now, his empty head nodding, straining to recall whether the train had a caboose?

He began typing again: persistent little memories, insertions for the first chapter. "The most uncomfortable memory of seventh grade at the Maplewood elementary school was being assigned by Mrs. Allen, the Science teacher, to work with Patsy Walnun on a physics experiment. If only she hadn't said it out loud. *Steve, please pair with Patsy on the soap bubble demonstration.* The boys in the class were pointing at him, smirking and making remarks, a few calling him Soapy."

He sat back and thought about what he had just written. How could he convert that into fiction? Who is doing the speaking about the seventh grade? Readers will ask: who is this Patsy person? Mrs. McFarland said there are techniques for character introduction to be covered in a later session. Okay, the Science class embarrassment could wait. There were some earlier events in his life that should be mentioned. He needed more details.

For a second time that evening as he sat poised over the keyboard, a realization took shape that he had walked the halls of that school for years and now could remember only an encounter or two with some colorless schoolmates, or unimportant activities like erasing the blackboard, or maybe running his finger over an earlier student's initials cut into his desktop. Was his memory really slipping away, subtly, the loss unnoticed? He felt the soft touch of panic. Memory loss? He hadn't planned on that. More reason to get material down on paper. More reason to go through that stuff that Alice sent.

The old box marked DAD'S in the garage held some secrets. It could be worth mining; there might be records of places he had visited with his father. Maybe ticket stubs from the ballgame where his father bought him a hot dog and a cap with the team name in white embroidery. Or there might be a flyer advertising the museum he visited with his mother to see the models of the sailing ships. He left the den.

As he passed the kitchen, he saw Evelyn sitting at the family room table, reading. She looked up. "I thought you were working on your book."

"I am. I need some reference material."

She raised her hand showing she got the message. Steve kept walking.

In the garage he pulled out the dusty carton from his sister and reached inside, touching objects at random. Something felt like a small, hard-covered album. He picked it up and held it to the side where the overhead light fell. The cover was labeled with gold lettering: *Our Family Photos.*

He grew curious. As he felt the smooth imitation leather binding, he knew his father's hand had touched the same cover where now his fingers traced the grain.

He opened the album. There was page after page of photographs, all black and white, about three by five inches, tucked in plastic sleeves. Most of the pictures were probably taken with his father's Kodak folding camera. He flipped the pages, stopping at one picture of his father and mother standing in front of a brick wall, somewhere, looking very young and cheerful. Was it nineteen twenty-six? There were some faded hand-printed words on the border: "Arthur and Julianna, the newly-married couple." The thought charged in: *Dad, I never asked you how you met mom or the year you were married.* That was a question never to be answered; anguish set in. He turned the page over.

The photograph dominating the next page was a full-length image of his father at a younger age, standing alone on a walk by a solitary tree, looking dapper in a straw hat, the style in the twenties. He had never seen this photograph, but he remembered the hat well.

It was typical day when he was a six-year old. He must have asked his mother if he could go out in the back yard to play; she had called to his father to get Steve's warm coat out of the closet. He had run to where his father was separating the garments dangling there. His father had paused his search of the coats hanging from the rack; instead he reached into the shelf above, saying "Hey, what's this?'. He pulled down a skimmer and handed it to Steve. "Here," he said "Try this on." The hat was made of a crisp, light yellow straw. The top and brim were flat with sharp edges. His father placed the hat on Steve's head; it fell over his ears, down to his eyebrows.

Steve lowered the album, reached up and touched his head as if the hat were still there. His father should have taken a photo of him wearing the hat. It would have fit well in the album.

His thumb flipped over the next page. The photograph on the left side was of a child, perhaps six months old. The child was posed on a furry blanket, wearing a near-white, very loose pair of pajamas. He assumed it was of him. As he was about to turn to another page, he saw the tiny lettering "Junior" in the lower right-hand corner.

This was not the baby Steven; this was the older brother that was never spoken about. His father was forever silent on the subject. It was by accident that he discovered there had been an earlier child, a boy. Sometime shortly after his fifth birthday, he had caught his mother going through a small box of infant articles: a rattle, a gown, a soft brush. The items were not his. He asked his mother who they belonged to. She answered in more of a tight-lipped manner than she probably intended. He almost regretted he had asked. She said sternly, "These things belonged to your baby brother. He died many years ago."

"How did he die?

"He had a bowel obstruction."

"Daddy never told me."

"I know. He felt very bad about it. Don't mention I said anything. I'm sure he will explain it to you sometime later."

He closed the album and dropped it back into the box, closed the lids, and returned to the den.

The empty, white page on the computer screen was waiting for him. He had to find some words that described the emotions brought on by the pictures— two people in the photo that he loved very much, that he really knew so little about. *Something* had to be written about them for God's sake. His hands dropped into his lap. The trip to the garage did not give him the inspiration he needed. The buoyancy he had experienced earlier that evening faded.

His hands came up and his fingertips tapped the keys nervously, uselessly. This wasn't going to work. There was no book! What the hell was he thinking?

The grandfather clock in the hallway chimed ten times. Evelyn had probably changed into her pajamas and was turning down the blanket on the bed. He shut the computer down, turned off the light in the den, and walked stiffly to the closet where he grabbed his nightwear off the hook. He went into the bathroom, brushed his teeth, and changed his clothes.

As he entered the darkened room, Evelyn raised herself to her elbows in the bed. She rolled over and switched on the lamp. "Earlier today I turned up the thermostat. I was cold."

"I noticed. I turned it down."

"Are you going to do some more writing tonight?"

"Nope. I ran out of ideas. The workshop instructor said morning was the best time to get over a block if one comes. I'll try again after I get up or after some breakfast."

The sheet caught his foot as he pushed himself over the edge of the bed and pulled the covers up to his chest. He looked up at the ceiling, briefly, then closed his eyes to experience the dark.

What was the wording of the book premise he concocted? *Elderly man learns . . . something.* His thought trailed off. Anyway, he could print it out and attach it at the top of the monitor. He might even run it by Mrs. McFarland.

His attention was drawn to the rhythm of his heart. It always seemed regular to him, but something had bothered his cardiologist when the stethoscope was pressed against his chest. Doctors were always suggesting tests. He will be fine. All he needed to do was relax. Breathe calmly. Tomorrow was definitely the start of the book. The action and the dialogue will come. But for now, the darkness.

BERNICE

HUMAN figures appeared around him. The dream began. He was sitting alone at a round table in The Select Cup. He didn't remember going there. A tall, white, paper tumbler half-full of steaming coffee was at his hand. He marveled at the visible detail of the rolled brim and of the swirls of vapor as they rose from the surface of the coffee. The place was filled with customers milling about and chatting—an unintelligible crackling sound.

The top of the table was a vibrant blue circle with a sharp white edge. Across the room, brushing the exteriors of the windows, were leaves, intense green in color, leaves of a tree he didn't recognize. Everything was crystal clear: the patrons, paintings hung on the walls, the silver coffee urns behind the counter. He thought he might be needed at home, but he knew of no reason to go there. Perhaps he was supposed to meet someone here, but he wasn't sure.

A body passing the table brushed him, and he turned to face a woman who positioned herself behind the chair next to him, seizing its back with a firm grip. Her head was slightly cocked. She had the look of someone who knew him for a long time, an old friend waiting patiently to be recognized. There was something familiar about her, but he could not place her features; should he? He was attracted to her hands. Her fingernails were nicely buffed, but without color. She wore a slight smile. He guessed her age as about forty. Her face was mature, well-proportioned, striking and severe, with a strong jawline. Her hair was short, slightly curled, and a bronze color, like her eyes. They were calm, confident eyes. Her brows were a lighter brown and thin. Her nose was narrow. Permanent smile lines were the only interruption in the smooth skin above and around her eyes and below her prominent check bones. The features of an actress.

His eyes were drawn to the animation of her mouth as she spoke. The pitch of her voice was low, and her words were carefully articulated as though she had rehearsed them. "I know I shouldn't be bothering you," she said with a glint in her eyes. "But I recognized you from the last time you were here." Pausing for a moment she added, "And there is something I *have* to say."

He was off his guard and completely puzzled. He smiled back. "Are you sure you have the right person?"

"Yes, you were conversing with the other, older gentleman, the one with the goatee—I guess you'd call it that." She laughed. It was not a giggle; it was laughter that celebrated years of enjoying and accepting peculiar differences in people. "I'll only take a few minutes of your time."

"I realize I'm getting forgetful as I get older, but we've never met, have we?"

"Never."

He found himself enjoying the give and take, her relaxed expression, the excitement of finding out who this person is. But the attention of an attractive woman was too odd. Was he being hustled? "I guess

I'm having a little trouble understanding why you're taking the time to stop by and talk. I'm nobody special."

"You said something that I connected with."

He knew there was a longer explanation coming. She moved side to side, eager to speak. His courteous nature took control. He said, "You're going to wear yourself out standing there; have a seat." He waved at the chair she had latched onto. At his signal she placed a zippered, floral-patterned pouch on the table, pulled the chair back, and hopped up.

She was wearing a dark blue denim jacket over a white top with thin, deep blue horizontal stripes. She pulled on the jacket collar to straighten and close it. "I know I must look like a hippie, but I didn't expect to run into anyone today."

He tilted his head. "I haven't heard that term in over forty years. I'm not sure I can recall what a hippie looks like."

She continued smiling, but sat silent, studying his face intently and patiently, as though she were deciphering his mood.

He waved at one of the baristas that was wiping a nearby table. The young man, clutching a damp white cloth in his palm, came up to Steve. "You need something?"

He looked back toward his attractive, very feminine guest and tapped his cup. "Care for some coffee?

"If you will be so kind."

Steve handed the young man a five-dollar bill. "Could I impose on you to bring a cup for this nice lady? She would like your Sumatra blend." The clerk took the bill, nodded and headed toward the coffee bar.

Steve leaned forward. "You've got me guessing. What did I say that engaged you?"

All at once she became very relaxed, completely comfortable in his presence. Her words came with great warmth. "You're very forgiving of my rudeness. I should introduce myself. My name is Bernice Batelle."

"I'm Steve."

"I know, I heard you mention your name during your conversation on Saturday. I didn't mean to eavesdrop."

"What else did you hear me say?"

"You said you were trying to get your ideas together for a book you're writing. I consider myself a writer of sorts and I know what you're going through."

"Are you in the publishing workshop? I didn't see you there."

"No. I've had all the writing classes I need. I should confess I'm working on a book myself. I have the material and the direction strongly in mind, but I'm stalled out. I've been ill, and on top of that arthritis is making the use of my hands difficult. You look healthy and ready to go."

"And you have some suggestions for me?"

"Yes."

"Well, the problem, Bernice, is that . . ."

She interrupted. "You can call me Bunny."

"Bunny?"

"That's a nickname I picked up in grade school."

"As I was about to say, Bunny, I've gathered a heap of advice on arranging the elements of a novel and creating a readable style, but I haven't been able to convert the advice to practice. I was hoping the workshop will pull things together for me."

Bernice looked away as if distracted. Steve guessed he was overstating his difficulties, monopolizing the time. There was more about her he wanted to know. "You say you have some writing you want to do, but you aren't up to it."

She nodded stiffly.

"What *are* you into?" he asked. "Romance? Maybe a murder mystery?" He smiled and chuckled.

She did not smile in return. She raised herself on her elbows a small amount, continuing her gaze in the distance. "I suppose I'm a little where you are. I, too, have memories I want to solidify—in words, that is."

"Don't women want to tell about the men in their life?

"Yes, there were some that were a strong influence. They came and went, mostly disappointments."

He placed his fingers to his lips. "Oops, sorry. Wrong topic. What about your childhood?"

Now she began to smile ever so slightly. "Yes. Little girls have many things to recall."

She paused, took a breath as if to strengthen herself to continue. "When I was about ten, my mom took me shopping often. We walked to all the stores. There was a women's wear shop we always passed on Central Avenue. In the window was a dress—my size. I fell in love with it. I wanted it for those important occasions." With that she fell back, looked skyward and chuckled softly. "As if there were any." Her face turned sober again. "I thought about that sweet dress every night when I went to bed. I can still see it now."

"It must have been special."

"It was. The fabric was a smooth, shiny pink. With a large hem. There was a big black bow on the front of the waistband." Her look grew stern; she placed her hand to her temple. "Pink was *my* color— it was me!"

Steve felt a comment was in order, but what? "I can see it was important to you. Did your mother know how much you wanted it?"

"Yes, she knew. I pleaded with her, but she said it was very expensive. She said she would try to put some money together to buy it for me. I wish she hadn't said that."

"Why?"

"I believed her. I saw myself wearing it. But I think she only said that to quiet me."

Steve hesitated to ask. "What then?"

"The next time we went shopping, my mother purposely walked on the other side of the street so I wouldn't see the dress. But on the way home she forgot and took the route that passed the store."

"And, of course, you saw the dress and you asked her if she was saving the money as she promised."

Bernice frowned. "The dress was gone from the window. I began to cry. My mother wanted to go home, but I was so overcome she took me into the store. The clerk said the dress was sold. It was the last one."

Steve asked, "Is that in your book?"

"Not yet." Her eyes darted downward, as though she were avoiding an unpleasant vision.

He smiled broadly, hoping to brighten the moment. "You may be having the same problem I'm having. There are a few bitter experiences I'd like to get off my chest."

"Tell me one."

"I think I was twelve. My school was trying to get everyone interested in gardening. They sold seed packets for just a few cents. I remember holding them, reading the instructions on the plain, little brown envelopes they were packaged in. There were carrots, radishes—easy things to grow."

"And you planted a vegetable garden."

"Yeah, I tried. The soil in our back yard was very dense and rocky, but I loosened it up. I had a couple rows of carrots and a couple rows of turnips. Everything sprouted. I was very proud."

"That sounds like a happy memory."

"It was until one day during my summer vacation. I was on my hands and knees, with a trowel, digging up some weeds near my crop. Everything was growing vigorously. The leaves were sturdy and green. A man, a next-door neighbor, was watching me. He leaned over the waist-high, chain-link fence that separated our yards. He was grinning, and, in a very rude and superior tone, asked me what was *wrong* with my garden."

"My God. Had you ever talked to him before?"

"No. I never saw him before that day. I was stunned. This was *my* garden and it was *beautiful.* Suddenly I couldn't think. I stopped, squeezed the handle of my trowel with anger, and looked down at the soil. I was asking myself why a grown man would say that to a child? At that moment it all became clear. He was letting me know he considered my garden a joke."

"What did you do?"

"I mumbled something like, 'well, when I get these weeds out, these plants will be fine.' I didn't look at him again, but I remember his smirk. I left the garden and went inside our house. I never hated anyone so much in my life."

The thought tightened his jaw. He had never told his father about the neighbor's comment. Why get him involved? He had enough to worry about—money mostly—like the time he overheard his father telling his mother they couldn't afford new curtains. Did he expect his father to go next door and punch the guy out?

"And you want to include that in your book?"

"That's one of the events, yes."

"To allow your mean neighbor to read about himself."

"I'm sure he's long gone. He probably died a horrible death." His mouth formed a wry smile.

"You probably have other unpleasant memories like that."

"Yeah, different times, different circumstances. I don't how to work them in." He felt he was repeating himself. "Maybe . . ."

Bernice raised her hand to quiet him. "You need some kind of template."

"A what?"

"You said you needed an excuse—some framework in which you describe your experiences, your memories."

She certainly had heard his conversation with Richard. He nodded. "That's right."

At his words she leaned back with a look of victory on her face. His agreement was obviously her sought-after prize. Her eyes went down to her pouch then back up to him. With firmness she said, "I have a pattern that'll work for you."

His eyebrows rose at her show of confidence. He bent forward and gazed at his clasped hands as if he were preparing himself for some revelation. The room became strangely quiet. He noticed the floor for the first time. It was a pattern of bright yellow tiles with splashes of black. That was not the way he remembered it when he sat with Richard.

The people at the tables had ceased vocalizing and were sitting motionless. Some had turned toward him, a sea of faces looking, listening. Were they all waiting for her answer? Did she have something meaningful to offer? Maybe it will be some obvious suggestion—*pretend it's a journal.* He had considered that version already and dropped it from his list. Whatever she came up with, he could always find some reason it wouldn't work and back off. But then it *might* work. Why not?

He asked, "What did you have in mind?"

She held up her hands in a time-out "T" sign and pursed her lips. "Let me back up. Have you picked a name for your main character?"

"I decided he will be Ray Gearland. My grandfather's name was Raymond. I made up the last name."

"How does he look?"

"What do you mean?"

"Describe him to me," she said, forcibly.

"Well, he looks like me."

"Fine, Now give me the words you will use to tell the reader about his appearance."

"You got me there. I haven't figured out how to describe characters yet. He's me. How would you describe me?"

Bernice leaned back and traced the curve of his face with her finger. "Are you listening?"

"Yes."

"Then remember what I'm about to say."

He had to admit she was comfortable giving orders. "Shoot."

Her face became expressionless as she scoured her mind for just the right adjectives. Her eyes had the look that Rembrandt must have had, staring at a blank canvas, conceiving a portrait, choosing the elements that defined it.

Speaking with conviction, she said, "Although he was getting on in years, Ray's face had many youthful traces. His hair was more than one shade of gray, with short tufts that pointed in all directions."

A group of two women and a man came by the table, waving arms and mumbling. Bernice ceased explaining, looked down, scowling. The trio hurried away. Bernice resumed her description. "His forehead was only lightly furrowed. His eyebrows were darker than his hair, angular, not curved. There was slight puffiness under his eyes. The flesh of his face was filled out. His lips were always firmly closed—straight across, but the lines above them created the appearance of a smile. The shape and movement of his dark eyes suggested he was observing more than thinking."

He rested his chin on his fist, not quite sure how to react. "I'm flattered. I'll try to remember all that. What about the pattern you had in mind? I'm waiting to be rescued."

"Very well then, this is the framework: throughout your novel, Ray tells a person—his close friend—about his memories. You know, he spills out his life. The friend is someone who has similar memories to deal with—and understands. They talk a lot about their lives. That way you get to relate *everything.*"

"Who is that person?"

"Me."

It occurred to him that what she was suggesting was more than a spur-of-the-moment solution. It came across like a sales pitch she had prepared well before she walked through the door of the shop and sat down across from him. But he felt himself buying in to her enthusiasm.

"You?"

"Yes, *me,*" Bernice said again as she jabbed and jabbed a well-manicured finger at the top button of her jacket.

"How does Ray come to be friends with you?"

"He meets me in a coffee shop."

"I'm not following you."

"Seriously, Steve, hear what I'm saying. When you go home and sit down at your word processor, or paper pad, or whatever, simply describe *our* meeting today."

"Such as?"

"Ray encounters this woman . . ."

Bernice raised her arms and gestured vigorously over the cups like a stage director. "Ray has coffee with her—in a place like this. He relaxes and gets comfortable. He tells her about something that happened to him at school when he was little, some incident that made him feel good—or bad. She considers his story very interesting."

She paused to watch his reaction, leaning toward him, looking straight into his eyes, speaking again, spacing her words carefully to add emphasis. "She begins sharing some of *her* memories, *her* fancies as well. Ray finds the woman to be a sympathetic spirit."

For a moment Steve is caught up in the script she is fashioning for him. Yes, it could work—but only for a chapter. He tossed his concern back at her. "I can't imagine a whole book based on a conversation over coffee."

His hesitation did not temper her positive attitude. She was very ready with a reply. "No, no. Writing that first scene is just to get your creative juices flowing. The setting and the interchange give your character, Ray, the opportunity to relate past events or feelings tied to the location where they meet, a place to insert his reflections on what he is telling the woman."

The muscles of his face tightened visibly in discomfort. "That's an awful lot of talk-talk."

Her voice became soothing. "It's not. You also describe what Ray is *doing*, what the woman is *doing*, what's going through his mind. It's not just dialogue."

"You mentioned something about a *first scene*. What did you mean by that?"

"The coffee shop is only the *first* encounter. Ray bumps into the woman in other places, maybe the library—she spends a lot of time in the library— or arranges to meet her to share some activity, you know—like an art sale. Each time they meet he tells her a little more about himself . . ."

Her voice trailed off; her face became somber. She added, "And she tells *him* about *her* fun times— and about the little hurts that came along—the baggage she has had to carry."

"Does she have a lot to tell?"

Pulling her shoulders back, she looked aside, clearly preparing an answer. "Yes," she said in a quiet growl. But no explanation came.

He found himself tracing the line of her jaw, the movement of her hair on the collar of her jacket. Her animated features were a pleasure to watch. Her spell was enveloping him. Her plan could work. It might just be possible that the finale of the novel he ached for was just months, perhaps weeks away. Her voice tone found a resonance in his ears and muffled the noise of the jumbled conversations building again around them.

But a tiny doubt arrived that interrupted the flow of her logic. It wouldn't be easy penning all of thoughts she was advertising. By evening he will be alone at the keyboard, straining to find the words that described this moment. That tiny doubt whispered for him to say "thanks" and wrap it up. But he couldn't let go.

"Well, Bunny, you've pointed out a way to, should I say, mechanize the process. I'd be willing to give it a try."

Her expression did not change. She must be experiencing victory, but thank God, she didn't applaud.

She reached across the table and touched his hand. "I know you, Steve. And I know you can do it."

The touch startled him. He held his hand still, controlling the instinct to pull it back. *I've just met this woman; what does she think she sees in me?* She is expecting too much. His arms went up, displaying his uncertainty. "I hope I can remember all this. I haven't been taking any notes as you can see."

The barest of smiles touched her mouth.

"When you describe our meeting, you don't have to be exact, Steve. You know what *this* place, this coffee bar, looks like; it will be an easy illustration for your readers. You know what *I* look like."

At these words he studied her face again. He noticed things he hadn't seen when she first took custody of his table. There was something compelling. He thought he read in her eyes and in the movement of her jaw something more to her nature than her few words revealed, more he wanted to know about.

"Okay, I'll begin my first chapter again—third try."

Bernice took a breath and grasped her pouch, checking the zipper. She scanned the area to her left and slid off the chair. Steve watched her descend safely, noting her matching dark blue jeans and black suede ankle boots with large, silver buckles.

As they walked out the door of the shop onto the rush on the breezy walkway, he found himself with more questions about her. He didn't want to exit the mall, leave her behind, still wondering how well he could get to know her—and how safe *was* it to know her better? That was not important. He had to focus on the book. What about bringing in other characters? Wait, what about *her*?" His voice rang with his anxiety. "Bunny, a quick question!"

She came to a stop, turned to him. "Sure."

"What is my friend's name?"

She hesitated. "Her name is Phyllis."

"Does she have a last name?"

"Well, we want something unique. Let's see. Yes, make it McKardle. Here, I'll write it out for you."

She unzipped her pouch and took out a small pad of paper. She printed the letters and held it up to Steve.

He nodded. "Got it."

She replaced the pad and looked at Steve, motionless, as if waiting for further questions.

He wanted to keep the conversation going, and sensed she did too. He extended his arm. "Well, we're partners now. I think we should shake on that."

She raised her hand which he grasped firmly, holding it for a long time, looking solemnly at her face. Her hand was relaxed; she didn't pull it away. It was though she had given it to him to keep.

"I'm going home now, Bunny. I'm going to write about us. I promise. By the way, do you need a ride?"

"No, I have my truck."

"A truck?"

"Yes, I have a pickup truck. It's what you might call an orange color—and it's beautiful. Maybe someday you'll get to ride in it." She winked.

She turned swiftly and walked away. He watched her disappear into the parade of shoppers; then he looked to find where he had parked his car. It could be in a hundred places; he couldn't remember. The image of the tree-lined lot faded.

In the morning sun, shadows of the huge white trumpet vine, tossed by the wind on the patio, raced across the bedroom drapes. The flickering daylight wakened Steve; he raised his head. Evelyn was still asleep. The braking squeals of the trash truck down the street grew louder. He let his head fall back. Traces of the dream lingered; there was a figure of a woman in jeans and a denim jacket. It was though he were still there in the coffee shop. *How did I get in bed?* He could still see her face; he remembered his last words: "Bunny, I'm going to write about us. I promise."

A TALE UNFOLDS

HUMMINGBIRDS circled and clashed for a perch on the feeder dangling from the white beam outside the den window. Steve looked up from the computer keyboard he was pounding to watch the aerial display. A shaft of sunlight from the eastern horizon, now a deep orange from its traverse through the liquid in the feeder, painted the wall next to him.

The small room in which he sat was another link in the chain of memories forged over the years. This had been the special bedroom set aside for Robert when Evelyn and he had brought their first and only child home from the maternity ward. Steve looked to his right where the crib had been placed, the one with the cute animal faces, the faces that amused the parents.

The room evolved as Robert grew. The crib was sold and replaced by a bed, his son's choice, with the appointments of a racing car: a steering wheel at the head, four tires, and a sloping front end. Then one day Robert joined the Navy as Steve had. He moved out and never returned.

The room evolved another turn. Evelyn installed wall-to-wall book shelves to house her growing collection of must-read fiction. A growth that never ceased. Then came the steel file cabinets, then the office desk, and in tune with the digital age, a computer desk and hutch found room next to the window.

The birds departed; he looked back at the screen, assessing the words he had typed: "Chapter One . . . A Soul-Mate Arrives". Would that work? Mrs. McFarland said that the title should tempt the reader's interest but shouldn't give away the essence of the chapter. *Hell, it can be changed later.*

As he looked at the cursor below the words on the screen, some choices began to nag him. His original plan yesterday had been to have his lead character, Ray, come across a high school year book he had bought as a senior. It could be found in a box in his garage, in the same way he had found his father's penmanship certificate. Ray will read the artless accounts, questions, penned in the margins when he was a naïve, unworldly young boy.

Or those comments and questions could have been jotted down in a diary. Why did Elsa Karch turn down his invitation to the Senior Prom? The word was out that she was dating *everybody*. He liked Mary Myerson; should he ask her?

Those simple words would set the stage for the unfolding of a lengthy memory that Ray pores over in his mind in graphic detail. That approach sounded good, but he knew it was trite. Ray's diary? There was never a diary. Besides, the diary gimmick has been overdone—a hundred times. Didn't he see Evelyn holding a book last month with the title *Diary of a Star*? That approach could get old, fast

Front and center in his herd of options, of course, was the somewhat complicated apparatus suggested by the visitor, Bernice, in the dream: Ray finds himself confiding in a total stranger, a woman at that! Would that be marketable? What about Ray's wife? Did he have one? Of course. He will have to reveal his new friendship with Phyllis to her; unless, of course, he was a widower. Would a potential buyer, a man like himself, who picked the book off the shelf, looking for some reading material he could relate to, make it past the first page?

Mrs. McFarland said that the reader will accept any premise if you treat it seriously and follow through with it. That defined his job—make the story real—as real as the words, the images, the sounds that carried over from the dream. The words were there and ready to flow. That was it: Ray meets Phyllis.

He began typing again. "Ray leaned on his cane to steady himself as he considered the prospect of a steaming mug of good coffee at the café down the walk." He liked that sentence—and the cane prop. The reader gets the message that Ray is older and a little bit unsteady. *How does Phyllis get introduced?*

Steve leaned back. This was another of those "artistic decisions" he had to make. A shopping center like the All-Traders Mall would be the place for her to appear. Ray meets her in the parking lot. Yes, she could be standing by an old pickup truck, dressed like a ranch boss, with arms crossed, frowning, looking first at the truck and then into the distance.

That could work. Other ideas were crowding in. Notes were needed; there was no time for narrative. Steve turned from the computer and slid a thick pad of paper over the mouse pad. He plucked a pencil from a cup and began writing brief phrases. Let's see. He will have Ray approach her and ask if she had a problem. She will say "yes", that her battery had died, explaining grimly that she had called the tow service, but was told the driver was finishing up another run. She turns to Ray, her eyes large and clearly agitated, raising her arms in despair, exclaiming, "They said it will be an hour wait!"

Steve paused the narration in his head to let the hand with the pencil catch up. This encounter should occur at the time of year when the wind whips up, giving Ray reason to suggest that she sit out the wait in the café, perhaps have some coffee with him. He assures her the tow truck, when it shows up, will be visible in the window. She accepts.

The pad was filling with pencil scrawls. Details were coming faster . . . her name . . . when should her name come up? It was natural at that point for Ray to introduce himself. "Just call me Ray," he offers. She responds, "I'm Phyllis."

The continuity to follow was clear in Steve's mind. *Ray accompanies her to the doorway of the café. They find an empty table. Ray starts to take a good look at this person he has just met. She is more than attractive; she is riveting.*

Steve stopped writing, underlined some words, and began writing again, fast. What was she like? He listed adjectives for her features, her clothes, her mannerisms. *Yes, there is some good stuff here.*

The words were coming too fast for a pencil. He put the pad aside, opened the manuscript on his computer to the first page, and began typing. This was rewarding; no, this was *excitement*. He wrote how, as Ray and Phyllis sipped their java, they commented, sometimes in amusement, on the peculiar variety of people types at the tables, the hypnotic, rhythmic swaying of the trees, and the recognizable shapes of the clouds they watched through the coffee shop window.

This was getting easy. Ideas for other topics for their conversation began springing up—like Phyllis's truck. Ray asked for details about her truck and why she drove one. She said that was her style.

At that moment, for Steve, it seemed everything in his endeavor was on his side; the tide was moving his way. There, right up in front of him, was his prodigious output of narrative for the day. Why had he doubted his ability to finish the book?

But—at that very moment—as his confidence began to swell, that funny, all too familiar uncomfortable feeling in his chest announced a visit. It wasn't bad, just a hint of an ache. He sat totally still, waiting, his chest motionless mid-breath. It was probably not his heart; he must have reached for something the wrong way. The significance of that tingle was that it served as a reminder of a lesson learned long ago: the moment you feel cocky about pulling off a great caper, that is the moment your good fortune puts on the brakes and goes the other way. That turn of the wheel would set him up for an ironic note in his obituary: "He was polishing the last few pages of a promising novel when the heart attack struck." What a shame. But very poetic, he thought: *Death came in a manner quite rude.*

He was becoming aware material was being added beyond the range of the dream. Things were being said that neither he nor Bernice touched on. Why not? Wasn't that the object of her "tell-a-friend" approach?

Footsteps interrupted him. Evelyn, eyes partly closed, pulling a robe around her shoulders, shuffled into the den doorway. "Hey, early bird, I didn't hear you get up"

"I tried hard not to wake you."

"Is that your book you're working on?"

He tapped on the pad. "Yeah. I have some notes here I wanted to get down, stuff that occurred to me when I woke up this morning."

She nodded approval. "Good. Want some breakfast?"

"I'd like to keep working. You could bring me a cup of coffee—maybe some toast."

She smiled, sleepily. "I can't. I'm going to my sister's place to have breakfast. Why don't you go out somewhere and treat *yourself* to a nice breakfast? What about that Select Cup you told me about?" She rubbed his back. "If you do go there, get some more of those scones."

He shrugged, pointing to the image on the monitor. "Maybe I will—can't promise. I want to finish what I started."

"I'm glad to hear you got over that hurdle. Are you using some ideas you got from the workshop?"

"Actually, no. I'm trying an approach I dreamed about."

Evelyn rubbed her eyes and looked at the ceiling to stretch her neck. "I've read that a lot of authors have used their dreams as a story plot. I'm trying to remember . . . yes . . . *Frankenstein* by Mary Shelley. There were some others. What happened in *your* dream?"

"It's involved. I'll tell you about it later." It wouldn't be easy explaining who the "friend" is that agreed to listen to his thoughts. Evelyn might ask why he chose Phyllis. Why didn't he invent somebody named Alec, a college buddy? A valid question. A reader might expect a bigger spark of comradeship with someone with whom you spent four years in class, four years studying for finals. The problem is that "Alec" will be a hell of a lot older now—as old as Ray—too old to care about anything other than his failing eyesight. Page after page, would the elderly Alec give a damn hearing about Ray's job as a bus boy in the lunchroom at the air base where his father worked, or the story of how he spilled the milkshake on the airman's uniform?

Evelyn shook her fists in the air with mock urgency. "Can't you give me a little hint?"

"My main character is a guy named Ray. That was my grandfather's name. You remember me mentioning him."

"But you never knew him very well."

"It's not about him. I'm just using the name. This is how it goes: Ray runs into people. He makes friends easily. He discovers they like to talk about their lives, their adventures, same as he." Steve felt that should suffice as answer.

At his words, Evelyn grew more alert. She entered the den and seated herself in the one other chair. She smiled to indicate she caught his drift. "And Ray is *you*."

"For now, yes. But we'll have to wait and see how the story goes. Maybe Ray will say and do things I never did."

She smiled, amused by some thought. "Maybe Ray will do things you *wished* you had done." She fell back in the chair in relaxed laughter.

He looked down at his notes as he spoke, grinning, "You mean I could correct all the mistakes in my life? Like the time my mother gave me some change to buy myself some Valentine's Day candy. When I got to the store, I saw a display of greeting cards next to the candy counter. I could have used the money to buy her a card that read 'Be my Valentine, Mom'. I bought the candy."

Evelyn rocked forward in her chair. "Exactly. In your novel you can have Ray buy his mother the greeting card."

He shook his head. "No, I want to play the hand the way it was dealt. I have to let the record show that I was selfish."

She placed her elbow on the desk, laid her head on her raised fist, and gazed at Steve thoughtfully. "I understand. But even as you spell out your misdeeds, aren't you secretly thinking that these confessions absolve you of the guilt that bugs you? Aren't you hoping the reader will let you off the hook?"

He didn't know how to answer. He had never thought about the book in those terms. "I guess I'd justify my honesty by saying I'm describing a human being—the good parts and the blemishes."

She took that as an answer and nodded again. "If you want, I can read parts of what you have written as you progress."

That wouldn't work. Not at this stage. The narrative hadn't yet fully explained how important a role Phyllis plays. "I have to get a better handle on where I'm going with this," he said. "What I've got this far may not make sense."

"Okay, Mr. Hemingway. I'll leave you alone with your muse."

The word struck a nerve. Muse? Something to think about. Is Bernice his muse? To get on with his writing he had to decide how much description will be Bernice's and how much will be Steven's.

Evelyn raised herself slowly from the chair, grunting softly. "I can't move as fast as I used to. I'm going to get dressed." She slipped quietly out the door.

He turned back to the computer monitor and gazed at what he had written, amazed at how fast and easily the words came. The narrative states he is deep in a conversation with Phyllis, telling her he has lived in this area most of his life. She mentions she once lived on Cloud Avenue when she was very little. She asks if he knows where that street is. The question pulls up a memory—one that had stayed buried somewhere for a long time.

Ray tells her that when he was ten, an old man carrying a basket of folded business flyers, followed by several other boys of Ray's age, stopped him and asked if he wanted to earn some money. He said "yes." The man explained that as his little group walked past the houses along the street, Ray and the other boys will be handed flyers from the basket. They will each ran up the entry walks of a house to slip a flyer in the mail slot or slide it in the doorframe. The pay was a quarter.

Little Ray agreed. At the end of the long block, with all of the flyers distributed, the man returned to his car and the other boys went their ways. Ray pocketed his twenty-five-cent piece. He looked up at the street sign overhead where he stood. It was Cloud Avenue.

Steve sat back and read what he had typed with a great sense of satisfaction. He had always wanted to tell the world about his first job, an obligation that took his lifetime to fulfill, and there it was, in front of him, on the monitor. This was working. He was able now to relate things, trivial as they might be, accomplishments important to him. *I have reported a small incident in my life that someone, somewhere, someday will read about. It is done!*

The realization filled him with a strong, almost light-headed awareness of the ecstasy of writing, of capturing an emotion on paper. His mood became a mixture of a need to celebrate and a need to forge ahead in the manuscript, bringing more material to life.

He chose the former; he decided to celebrate. Evelyn said she wanted some more scones. He would purchase them when he got some hot coffee at the Select Cup and drank a toast to himself. If Richard were to show up, although not likely, he would tell him how great the writing was going; they could celebrate together.

He shut down the computer, picked up the jacket draped over the office chair, and walked out the front door to his car at the curb.

The traffic was light; a few minutes later he stepped into the bustle of the All Traders mall. The mall was busy, filled with the swarms of Sunday shoppers. The city had grown measurably since he and Ev moved there. There were more stores to visit, and more lines to wait in. Or maybe it just seemed that way as he grew old.

A group of six people stood blocking the entrance to The Select Cup, some waiting silently, some debating their choices of staying or moving on. The crowd was an omen, a sign that this was the wrong hour to get service. He walked around them and through the door to encounter more people packed inside. Every table, every seat he could see was taken. Two customers near him were giving up their table. A good sign. Two more women closed in, quickly taking their place.

A distant voice rose above the chatter. "Hey, Steve. Over here."

He turned to the sound. A man occupying a bench seat by the window had his arm in the air, motioning for Steve to come. Was the signal directed at some other Steve? He looked to the left and right; no one else was responding. The man kept fanning the air with his palm. Steve started moving, maneuvering past the occupied tables to where the man sat. As he reached the table, he tapped his chest, asking with a smile, "Are you looking for me?"

A man with a gaunt face smiled back at him and began spilling out questions faster than he could react. "Hey, aren't you the famous Mr. Ribman? How have you been, and what the heck are you doing these days?"

Steve remained silent, backing away slightly.

The man held out his right hand. "You're looking at Ron Cornwal. You must remember me. I ran into you a several times at the rec and park district. It was quite a few years ago."

Squinting, Steve said, "You look a little familiar, but I can't place you."

"I know, I've weathered a lot since I left. How about having some coffee together?"

The man he was sizing up must have played a role in a very remote period of time at the office, now a foggy flashback. Another clue that he was forgetting things, a disturbing reminder. Even so, it would be harmless to show interest. "Coffee," he said, nodding. "That's what I came for."

Ron slapped the leather of the bench. "Have a seat."

Steve slid in behind the low, rectangular table, collapsing next to this fellow of questionable background. Even though their paths may have crossed, it may have been under unpleasant circumstances. A brief glance confirmed his questioner was clean-shaven, had a recent haircut, and was wearing a tailored suit.

Ron waved for a waiter, then stared at Steve. "I was the maintenance director. You stopped by my office about every three months. Is it coming back?"

Steve watched the agitation in Ron's jaw as he turned away, waved again, calling to a young man in an apron carrying a tray. There was something in the voice, not the face, that was recognizable.

Steve gestured weakly, acting interested. "I think so. You're referring to the times I had to get some budget numbers from you. God, that was many, many years ago, Ron. You were a bit different then."

"Exactly. You've changed a little yourself," he said. "But for the good of course." He laughed.

A waiter, a slight man, with an olive complexion stepped up and bent over them. "Gentlemen, your orders please."

Ron, with raised brows, turned to Steve. "Your call."

"Whatever is on tap. The high octane."

Ron pointed to the brewing machines at the bar. "Today's dark roast. Two large cups."

The waiter disappeared.

Ron placed his elbows on the table, his chin resting on his folded hands. "Are you still with the district?"

"No—retired. But they asked me to stick around, part time."

"So, what are you doing with your retirement? Writing an expose of an over-funding scandal at rec and park?"

A grim expression crossed Steve's face. "I don't think we ever had to answer for over-funding. Money was always tight. There was that year we couldn't afford a lousy fireworks display on the fourth."

Ron nodded. "And I don't think anyone was ever overpaid."

"If I recall rightly," Steve said, "you were there for only about a year."

Ron's expression became somber. "It didn't work out for me. I found a better job with the county—they also needed a maintenance manager. The work is tough, but under control. I expect to be there for a couple more years."

Steve confided, "I could have hung in for a lot longer, but it dawned on me there was no reward for keeping at it until I keeled over at my desk. My wife is getting on. I wanted to spend more time with her. . . and . . ."

Ron interrupted. "Play a little golf."

Steve knew he could go on with this friendly, pointless conversation indefinitely, but the option to relax, reveal some personal details, and draw him into his circle of reverie was tempting. "I have no hobbies or fun things. However, to be truthful, I *am* writing a book—about my life, my marriage—a little about my years in the office."

"The office, too? That should be interesting." Ron leaned forward, smiling slyly. "Be sure to put in a few words about Lundery."

At the word *Lundery* an uncomfortable tension ran down Steve's arm. The name shook him, like a blow to the head, triggering a vision of an office milieu that he thought he had buried. He was annoyed and it probably showed in his question. "Why do you say that?"

"I shouldn't have. It's just that I had a lot of personal issues with John Lundery. He was the reason I left." Ron paused for a moment, twisted in the seat, then continued. "Actually, it wasn't just about me; he could have been the ruin of the whole organization."

The waiter returned with two large paper cups of a steaming deep brown liquid. "Your coffee, gentlemen."

Ron looked at the small receipt, tossed some bills on the tray. The waiter nodded and backed away.

"He died, you know," Steve said.

"Yes, in nineteen eighty-eight. I caught the obituary."

Steve began to think about some of his severe confrontations with John Lundery, musing over the fact that he never spoke about them to anyone—even Evelyn. Now, here was someone who probably shared the same pent-up resentment that Lundery was able to easily ignite.

"Yes, I endured a few bitter moments with Lundery," Steve said. "Was he on your case a lot?"

"Always. Sometimes we argued over major policy issues, but many times he harped at me over trivial things."

"That's the way I remember him," Steve said.

Ron raised a finger. "Once he came back from lunch, roared into my office, ordered me to get some old guy kicked out of the park. He said he had seen him there twice—he knew this guy was some kind of commercial photographer, working there without a permit, taking pictures of models."

Ron, his arm tense, began tapping his cup on the table. "When I asked why he didn't have the park ranger on duty talk to the man, he got even more furious. He said he couldn't reach a ranger; he wanted me, *personally,* to handle it."

Steve watched Ron tighten up, take short breaths as he spoke. "So, I drove to the park and checked the guy out. Listen to this, Steve; he was a nightshift manager at one of the local restaurants. The so-called model was his daughter."

"How did you break that news to Lundery?"

Ron's head bobbed. "I didn't. I simply said I told the man he had to go through a registration procedure. Lundery didn't like to be told the truth. He said he *knew* for certain the photographer was a professional because he was using a tripod, for chrissakes."

"Even so, how did Lundery know he wasn't registered?

"That's where it gets good," Ron said, chuckling. "Lundery made it a point to find out early about *anyone* who was legally shooting pictures in the park. He *arranged* for them to present him with some beautiful black and white studies of trees, clouds, picnickers. He had some in his office and even in his home."

Steve smiled. "I remember seeing them in his office—framed, under glass, really striking. I never made the connection."

As though he already knew the answer, Ron asked, "Did you have many run-ins with him?"

A vision of office settings with Lundery came to Steve, visits by the great leader that had him clenching his fists. "To be sure. The last go-around with him was over some trips he had me taking. He had been invited to participate in a series of meetings being held by some recreation and park association. He directed me to attend in his place."

Ron smiled, intentionally insincere. "Well, you got to take some trips."

Steve smiled in return, then grimaced. "There was a hell of a lot more to it than that. The rec and park group had initiated a study on cost reductions. They needed input from districts around the country. In the meetings, the chairman assigned each of the representatives, including me, to gather data on expenditures."

"Like maintenance."

"Exactly, but that took time. When I returned from the first meeting, Lundery asked me what I was doing. When I tried to explain I was working the assignment, making sure I made our district look good, he flat-out told me I didn't have time for that, and to stop."

"Did you?"

"I had to. Lundery would have found out I was quizzing all the departments for cost data. When I returned to the next meeting I went in empty-handed. That made me look bad."

"There was your chance to portray the kind of superintendent he was. Did you announce that you were *ordered* by him to stop the effort?"

"Hell, no. One of the vice-presidents of the association might have called him the next day, moaning about his lack of support. Lundery would have accused me of trying to torpedo him. I could see him calling me in to the office, closing the door, shouting in violent terms how I should have made up a story."

"So, you took the fall."

"Yeah, I *made up* a story. In the next meeting of the group I said everyone at our place was working overtime on analyses of a re-organization."

"I guess that's one episode you won't put in your book."

"Maybe I will, maybe I won't. If I do, I can't use real names of course."

Steve's attitude suddenly brightened. "You know what, Ron. I have been allowing those brushes with John to poison my life. I was bitter that I had the terrible misfortune to end up under his thumb. But it occurred to me, just now, as we talk, that I owe him a debt of gratitude."

"How's that?"

Steve cocked his head; his lips drawn tight to suppress a laugh; his palm extended to signify an offering. "He has supplied me with a basketful of potential material for my book."

Ron smiled. "You got it."

Steve raised his cup. "What do you say, Ron, let's drink a toast to John Lundery for his contributions to my life story."

Ron lifted his empty cup to his forehead. "I'm for that. By the way, what's your book's title? Now that I know where you're headed, I've got to buy a copy."

"I don't even have a working title."

Ron worked his way from under the table and off his seat to stand erect. He wagged his finger at Steve. "Okay, I'll keep asking at the book store for something by Steven Ribman. Is there some way we can stay in touch, so I'll know when the book is out?"

"Give me your card. I'll call—but it may be a long time."

Ron pulled out his wallet and let it fall open. He lifted a business card carefully from one of the pockets and handed it to Steve.

"Here's where you reach me. It's been great running into you. I have to leave. I have an appointment with destiny."

"Don't we all," Steve replied.

Ron walked away; Steve took one last glance around the coffee shop and headed to the front door.

STORY FIVE

QUESTIONS

MRS. McFarland was sitting in a folding chair at the front of the long room, watching the class members file in and noisily pull chairs out to take seats. Next to her was the large whiteboard on which she had written MAJOR AND MINOR CHARACTERS. Steve took his usual place at the front table. He looked around at the assemblage behind him. Last week he had kept his vision forward, focused on the introductory words of Mrs. McFarland; this week he paid more attention to the makeup of the class, particularly the women.

He thought about Bernice. In the dream she had told him she had taken all the courses she needed. Were there any like her here? He looked at the men. Were any there of his age, filled with his need to tell about some of those moments in his life, overflowing with excitement or, with gritted teeth, to admit to some failures?

When everyone was seated and the room became reasonably quiet, Mrs. McFarland rose from her chair. In her right hand was a book. Steve couldn't see the title. With her left hand she pointed to the words on the whiteboard and began speaking.

"At the risk of being accused of having a disorganized presentation, I'm going to digress a little from my planned first topic this morning."

She tapped the whiteboard. "Last week a couple of you, on your way out, had questions about character development." A voice from the side said "Yes."

She nodded and continued. "I realize that there are several people here who have interests other than fiction, such as Dr. Dohlstram back there." She waved. Steve turned and watched his new confidant wave back. "Dr. Dohlstram tells me he is writing a technical book. From what he has told me, I personally think it has the potential for a great novel, but I can't convince him." There were a few quiet laughs.

"So, I beg his indulgence while I try to answer that special question." She tapped the whiteboard again. "I was asked to state the rule on deciding how much of a role a character should play. And, yes, how much description does a character deserve?"

Her last words prompted Steve to look up from his notes. *How apropos!* Precisely what he was going to ask. He had given Phyllis a place in his book. Wouldn't it be more tactical, reader-wise, to exploit her for a few more discussions, then move on to other characters who willingly give him their ear for a while? Phyllis has served her purpose.

Mrs. McFarland went on. "I assume that you have chosen your main character. Now you have to decide how round and flat that character will be. But we'll get to that later. When it comes to minor characters, you also have to decide whether a central part of your story revolves around them, or are they put in simply to make a plot point."

Mrs. McFarland held up the book she was holding at her side. "I'm not going to try to give you the full answer today. We will go into that in a later session. I have a book here devoted to the topic of character development. I've clipped several pages. I ask those who need some immediate guidance to take a look at how various authors have handled that problem. You might just want to get a copy for yourself. I've arranged for the book to be available at the college book store." She laid the book on a small table near her chair, then turned, faced the class, and brought her palms together, chest-high.

"Today I'm going to cover what is known as creative non-fiction." Someone down the table from Steve murmured, "I'll go for that."

Steve wrote a few words in his notebook, and looked out the window at a faded blue banner, twisting in the breeze. The subject matter had no interest for him.

The instruction continued. There were words and lines added to the whiteboard; there were questions and answers. The morning dragged on for Steve.

When Mrs. McFarland announced that the end of the class had arrived, Steve immediately worked his way to the clear space alongside the tables and strode briskly to where Richard was seated, writing a few last words in his portfolio. He laid the pencil down and looked up.

"Steve, you're about to tell me you're ready for a hot cup of coffee at our favorite café."

"Definitely, Richard. I was thinking I might get more help from you than I did from the class today."

The two men joined the group leaving the building.

At The Select Cup, many customers, entering and leaving, filled the doorway—a disturbing sign for

Steve. Fortunately, Richard was able to take possession of a table while Steve ordered two coffees. Steve returned, placed a paper cup in front of Richard, and sipped from his own. Steve spoke first. "Well, how's your treatise coming along?"

Richard's voice was solemn. "I didn't do much writing; In fact, I don't even have a title yet. I'm struggling with that. I spent the week sorting my material. I took McFarland aside before the class started today and she gave me some tips on making the preface more engaging. There are a lot of books out there on sleep disorders. She suggested the preface has to explain why my book is different. How about you? Are you making any progress?"

Steve was ready with an answer. "Yes, as a matter of fact."

Richard slapped the table and fell back in a show of relief. "Glad to hear that. You asked me last week if I had any suggestions on how you might set up the incidents about your life you have in mind. I'm sorry; I couldn't come up with any."

Steve recognized the wisdom of staying silent about Bernice, but the temptation to relate a good story was too much. Surely Richard has heard stranger ones. "That's all right. I have a plan."

"What's that?"

"You won't believe this, but I got an idea from a dream. I have a direction now and I'm coming up with some good stuff. The end is in sight."

Richard's mouth closed tightly; his fist went up to his chin. He seemed torn between relaxed belief and reasonable skepticism. Steve smiled, pleased at how he was able to put the issue to rest with such finality.

Richard came alive again. Maybe he didn't buy the explanation. "Let me guess. You met Marcel Proust and he instructed you on how to write a book like *Remembrance of Things Past*."

"No, it's stranger than that."

Richard suddenly seemed intensely interested. He leaned into Steve. "Wow, the dream must have made a powerful impression if you're now able to write a whole novel. What were the circumstances?"

"The dream begins with me, alone, at this very table. A woman walks up and begins talking to me about my book."

The look of interest on Richard's face grew more pronounced; his eyes opened wider. "Someone you know?"

Steve surmised that Richard's instinct for gathering data was kicking in. "No, I never saw her before."

"Are you sure? Did she look a little like Mrs. McFarland?"

Steve wasn't sure whether he should laugh or harden his look. "You're kidding."

"A little," Richard admitted. "Although anything's possible. Was there even a *small* resemblance?"

"No," Steve said firmly. "That I'm sure about. It's amazing. I can remember her features as sharply as I can see yours now. I'd recognize her in a crowd."

"Was she good-looking?"

"Well, not what you'd call beautiful. I consider beautiful women to be cast from the same mold. Her face was distinctive—maybe there *was* a trace of seductiveness."

Richard didn't hesitate with his next question. "How old was she?"

"I put her age at late thirties, maybe forty-something."

"Was there anything familiar about her appearance or clothing?"

The probing was getting overly detailed and unnecessary. Richard was trying to find a clue to a woman who didn't exist. There was no point in further describing the outfit Bernice wore, which he *did* remember quite well. Sharing that clarity might raise suspicions that there was another woman in his life.

"Well, her outfit *was* unique," he said. "Maybe I should call it individual. I remember everything she wore; the details were sharp."

Steve waved at the widely scattered clusters of people standing and sitting. "She didn't dress like any of these women."

Richard took the cue and glanced where Steve was pointing. Near them was a young woman with a male friend. She had on black pants and a pure white shirt with the sleeves rolled up. A chubby woman wearing a yellow dress with a boat neck was breaking a cookie for her child.

Richard fell back, his head angled like a dubious detective in a movie. "When did you have this dream?"

"Last Sunday, early morning."

"Was it lucid?"

"I'm not sure I know what you mean."

"A lucid dream, Steve, is one in which you are *aware* that you are dreaming.

"Is that possible?"

"Oh, yes. But they're not very common. There have been a lot of studies on that mode of dreaming, but I never followed up on them. You'd know if it was lucid. Forget I asked the question."

Steve took him at his word and did not answer. Richard opened his portfolio and began making notes. Steve used the opportunity to revisit the mental image of the dream that stood out so strongly, to compare it to the people and the furnishings of the building that encircled him. He rubbed his hand over the top of the table, testing its solidity, noting that the colors were identical to those in his dream.

He interrupted Richard's writing. "I have to say again how incredibly real the dream was. It was though it *was* my life, not the life I'm living, sitting here, speaking to you."

"I believe you. Which brings up an interesting philosophical subject."

"What's that?"

"Think about this, Steve." Richard waved his arm at the collection of busy talkers and coffee drinkers that surrounded them. "What you consider to be life—the people in this room—that you call reality—are not actually what you see. We are surrounded by clumps of mass, which in turn are energy at the core. Those "things" out there generate sensory data that you interpret as people. Dreams are also the product of sensory information sent to your brain. So, which is 'real'? The stuff you call life—or dreams?"

"That's heavy, but I see what you mean."

Richard rapped the table to make a point. "The dream situation you described sure sounds like it was connected with all the advice on novel writing you're being fed. Think about it, Steve; maybe it *was* someone in the workshop."

Weary of repeating himself, Steve let his head tilt down, offering a negative nod until he was sure Richard got the message.

Richard, in turn, bowed to acknowledge Steve's belief. "Okay, then. It could be someone you met— even briefly. I really think it's a woman you saw on television, or in a photograph. You remembered the face and you've re-created it in your dream."

As the sunlight's direction shifted, it became a blinding glare, beams reflecting across the room onto the patrons from glass-covered fake paintings of steaming coffee cups on the walls. Reacting, Steve closed his eyes briefly to think. A sharp image of Bernice arose—she was there, right before him. He watched the replay of her emotions as she lectured him. He felt the emphasis added to her words by her body movement. He should confess to Richard that there is more that identifies her than a face. He had never known anyone as forceful.

The workshop? There had been no interchange with *any* of the women in the workshop that foreshadowed the relationship he found himself in with Bernice. She was too compelling. But that will have to remain unsaid. Richard might suspect there was a dalliance with her that goes beyond a dream.

"I *did* do a little thinking about the possibility of the dream being linked to the workshop," Steve confessed. "This morning I looked *very carefully* at all of the women in the class. There was absolutely no resemblance."

Richard appeared to accept his report, looking down to put his mind to the puzzle; He toyed with a button on his tan cardigan, then said, "This may sound like a strange question, and if it's not too personal, answer me this—did any concern cross your mind, in the dream, that word might get back to your wife that you were seen having a very personal discussion with a strange woman at the coffee shop?"

Steve perked up at the subject, aware of his unexplained acceptance during the dream of having no other relationships. "Actually, not a single thought occurred about anyone else in my life—my wife, my son, or friends."

Richard came back again quickly. "Have you talked to *any* women about your book?"

"Only my wife, Evelyn—and Mrs. McFarland."

"Did this dream-woman say how she *knew* about *your* book?"

"She overheard us conversing."

Richard, agitated, began sliding his cup in a circle on the table. "Let me get back to what you said earlier. What is the plan for your book that you gained from this dream?

Steve was pleased that the question was asked. "The main character—I named him Ray—meets someone who he discovers is willing to listen to him talk about his life." He watched Richard's reaction as he answered.

"Wait, how does this woman in your dream play into that idea?

"She suggested that *she* be that person. She wants my main guy to bump into her now and then. When they do, they spend time gabbing, reminiscing."

"Run that by me again. You say *she* wants to be the *only* person your main character interacts with throughout the whole novel?"

"Yeah, but I was thinking about inserting a few additional friendly people—maybe someone like you."

Richard blinked, raised himself up, and adjusted the collar of his sweater, as if preparing to receive a medal. "I'm honored," he said. "But let's proceed. When did this dream occur? In the middle of the night?"

Steve remembered the strange mixture of sensations when dawn illuminated the bedroom. He had lain there with closed eyes, still seeing Bernice, and feeling the pillow under his head.

"Early morning," Steve replied. "Just as the dream ended, I woke. It was about seven-thirty a.m."

Richard raised his hand over his portfolio and imitated a scribbling motion. "Did you write down the details of the dream?"

"No. Why all these questions?"

"One more," Richard said. "You say you remember all of the details?"

"The dream was very clear, more vivid than any dream I've ever had. When morning came, I remembered everything—and kept thinking about it throughout the rest of that afternoon."

"That's very strange."

"What is?" Steve asked, trying to catch up with Richard's train of logic.

"Almost all dreams fade from a person's memory as the day goes on," Richard explained.

Reaching over and tapping on Richard's expensive notebook, Steve asked, "Have you ever run into anyone in your line of work—helping people with their sleep problems—who was strongly affected by a dream?"

"Well, dream analysis is not my specialty. There were a few people we worked with who *mentioned* dreaming, but it wasn't related to their treatment." Richard ceased his delving and directed Steve's attention to a clock on the wall above a coffee urn. "Time is fleeting."

Steve eased off his chair. "Can you think of any other sources where that person, and the lecture she gave me, came from?"

"I think she was somebody you once knew— that you've forgotten. Maybe the woman represents a school teacher you had in an English class, a teacher that was trying to help you write an essay."

Steve took one last swig of coffee. "I'll probably never know. It doesn't matter. What do you think of the plan?"

"Well, at least you have a plot of sorts. Your guy, Ray, bounces his ideas, his memories, off people in his life during those moments of give and take that come up; that's workable. And you made the right judgement; you can't have Ray confessing to the same woman every day. The reader's going to think she's his analyst."

"So, you think it might work?"

"There's one issue," Richard said, his brow furrowing a little." Your protagonist, if you don't mind my using McFarland's ten-dollar term, needs to have a problem to resolve. There's no tension."

"That's the same word my wife used. I'm at a loss. What kind of conflict could arise in this situation?"

Richard shrugged "If I say any more, I'll be writing your novel. *You'll* have to deal with that."

"I will; let's go."

Both men threw their empty cups in a large wastebasket on the way out.

As Steve rolled into his side of the garage, he noticed Evelyn's car was gone. Probably shopping. It was just as well; she will have another long list of questions about the class. He grasped his notebook from where it rested between the seats and left the car.

On the desk in the den was a small pile of the day's mail. He tossed his notebook over the envelopes, scattering them, then fell into the office chair. The afternoon light was brighter than usual, as though the Earth was falling into the Sun. Covering his eyes, he raised himself and closed the shutters on the den window. He reached for the power button to activate the computer, hesitated, and, instead, looked down at his notebook, opening it where it had been clipped. The page was filled with a list of topics he planned to use in Ray's exchanges with Phyllis. He looked back at the monitor and began typing.

In the week after the dream, the writing had been proceeding surprisingly well. It was becoming almost mechanical: In page after page he has Phyllis make a comment about something she had seen happen or read in the newspaper. Ray responds to her comment with some mundane but positive appraisal, then launches into a long story about an incident in his life that grew from the kernel she offered.

Phyllis had become a useful tool. Why hadn't he thought of creating her earlier? Maybe he had. Maybe the idea had been lingering for years in his subconscious and finally worked its way out through the dream. But why waste time on that theory? Steve opened his notebook and looked at the dozen places where he had scribbled her name. Here, here, and here were scraps of dialogue gleaned from her lips. Enough to build half a novel around. Maybe too many?

He thought over what the learned Dr. Dohlstram had warned about. The overuse of Phyllis will become evident after a couple of chapters. Surely, he could find another equally interested ear. Steve thought about his years in the Navy, they were short, but they were a transformation in his life.

He could make Ray a veteran, an old salt. Steve wrote the words "sea stories" in the notebook. Yes, Ray could discover that Al Haddock, his buddy from boot camp, had moved into town. They had a lot of stories to share. That could do it. At the rumble of Evelyn's car, he closed the notebook.

Evelyn entered the room and dropped a stack of five books on the desk loudly. Steve looked at the stack and then at his wife. "What's that?"

"Could you run two errands for me?"

"I'll try. What are they?"

"I called the Anna Vail Senior Center. Their lecture program schedules just came in. You know, the talks on exercise, cooking, quilting—the stuff you don't like."

"And you want me to pick one up."

"Yeah. And drop off these books at the library next door. I'm donating them."

Steve placed his hand on the books. "I'll do that now. I was planning to visit the library anyway."

He lifted the stack and carried it into the garage. He opened the front passenger door of his white SUV and laid the books on the seat. His fingers found the small, black remote on the workbench and pressed it. The roll-up doors hummed and moved skyward as he eased through the door into the driver's seat. The engine started quietly, and the car rolled back into the driveway. The street was empty; he headed west.

Inside the library entrance, sitting near the wall, was a large wooden crate. Leaning against it was a piece of white cardstock that read DONATIONS. He bent over the crate and added his five books to the collection filling the bottom. He straightened, took a breath and looked into the long rows of shelves lined with book spines that seem to go on forever under the warm fluorescent lights. Surely among the thousands of volumes pressed side by side there must be one written by someone of no great talent, like him, a tale tracing a young boy's struggle to take hold of the reins of life.

Up ahead, to his right, a young woman in a beige jacket was sitting alone behind a long counter, looking intently at a computer monitor. A gray-blue label plate resting at one end of the counter identified it as the reference desk. He walked briskly to the woman. A small, oblong plastic badge pinned to her left shoulder read "Miss Wilkins." Steve confronted her, hesitating before he interrupted her trance. Her lips were pursed; she nervously brushed some brown curls from her temple as she leaned toward the monitor. She sensed his presence, turned up to him, smiled.

Steve leaned on the counter. "I don't know how to phrase this question. I'm looking for a book—or books—where the main character, a man, does a lot of thinking about the events in his life—events that have strongly influenced him. Do you have any suggestions?"

She put her hand to her chin and thought awhile before she answered. "There probably are, but I'm ashamed to admit most of my reading has been limited to books about women—by women authors."

He shrugged. "I suppose it shouldn't matter, but I'm guessing a woman's memories fall into categories different than those of a man. You know, a woman might think back about a dress she always wanted when she was little."

The woman reached for a small tablet of paper and slid it in front of her. She picked up a pen next to her keyboard and tapped it on the pad. "Well, men and women might share *some* concerns. Were you thinking about the stream-of-consciousness style?"

"What's that?"

"The reader gets to see what the character is thinking, rather than doing. The first one that always comes to mind, of course, is *Mrs. Dalloway* by Virginia Woolf."

"That really doesn't describe what I had in mind. Any other suggestions?"

She began jotting on the pad. "This book is a collection of writings—short stories actually—by women authors. It's an old one. There are several pieces where the characters are drawn into their past. Let's see, the book title is *Precious Moments Recalled.*"

She handed him the slip. He thanked her and inserted the folded paper into his wallet. The book could be looked into on another day. He strode to the entrance; the olive-tinted automatic doors slid apart disclosing a courtyard montage of library patrons in the late afternoon sunlight studying a large poster resting on an easel.

He began walking toward his car. The chatter he heard from the group facing the announcement aroused his curiosity; he turned and joined them. He had ignored the sign on his way in. Now he decided to find out what the attraction was. There was a colorful image of a book; the cover art was a small boy looking down a city street at a line of garish automobiles of the fifties—bright colors, bulging headlamps, tail fins, prominent grills. Below the cover was a man's photograph. Further underneath, the words "Kenneth Bretsom signs his new best-seller, *Rewalking My Path.*"

How about Steven Ribman's world-acclaimed novel? He could see another small crowd, in this very spot, in a few months perhaps, looking at *his* poster inviting them to *his* book signing. He had a very flattering portrait recently shot that could work for the poster, the one the recreation and park district had picked up the tab for—the one hanging in their "Hall of Distinguished Retirees". He looked again at the image of the book. Good art. Good title. He could have used both.

A small, elderly woman wearing a loosely-knit gray shawl standing next to him tapped on the poster. "I bought his book a month ago. If I had known he was coming here, I would have waited to get his autograph. It's a good book."

Steve looked down at her as she wagged her head nervously, expressing her disappointment. He raised his hand to get her attention. "What did you like about it?"

"He writes about his life. Nothing unusual—his school days, first jobs, stuff like that, but he describes them in such funny, interesting ways."

"How did you find out about it?"

Her eyes scanned his face, assessing this person who was delving into her private interests. "I belong to a book club. *Everybody* in the club bought a copy." Unfortunately, it was not Evelyn's book club.

A vision crossed his mind—a lively group of ladies seated and standing in a living room, sipping tea, asking each other what they knew about this new author, Steven Ribman. Maybe they would invite him to speak about his book. They might coax him to reveal a few luscious incidents that he had judiciously left out.

He gave the woman's shoulder a slight nudge. "If I wrote a book about *my* life, would you buy it?"

"Well, if it was written as good as his, sure. Some people are attracted to true stories; I know *I* am."

He said no more. A few more people crowded in to read the description. The little old lady with the gray shawl wobbled away toward the lane of parked cars. He looked again at the poster. What a coincidence. Someone else writing about his life. Maybe this was the helping hand of fate. There might be a few ideas for getting memories on paper waiting for him inside

Steve walked back to the entrance. The gray doors opened, and he stepped into the cool interior. Across the entry area from where he had dropped off Evelyn's books was a short, wooden stand. Taped at the top was a small, white square of paper bearing a crudely drawn arrow pointing to his left, with the words BOOK SIGNING. He turned toward where the arrow directed. Up ahead, a cluster of people were entering a room. He continued down the hallway to the gathering.

From the doorway, looking into the room, he could see visitors picking up books from stacks on the table where a man was seated, a man that matched the photograph in the poster outside the building. The skin of his face was taut, he had a full head of hair. Mature but not very old. Had he lived long enough to have memories worth telling?

One of the visitors, an older man with tussled white locks, was leaning over the author, commenting and gesturing emphatically. Steve walked inside and stood close to the exuberant talker. The man paused, smiled, nodded at Steve, and stepped back. The seated man looked up at Steve. He rose slightly and offered his hand. "Hi, I'm Ken Bretsom."

"I'm Steve Ribman. Is that your real name or a pen name?"

Ken laughed. "Well, that's the name on my birth certificate. Have you read any of my books?"

"No, but I bumped into one of your fans outside. She said you have a captivating way of describing your life."

"That's encouraging. I think Jean Shepherd does a better job, but I try.

A young woman came up and held a book at arm's length. "I'd like you to sign my copy, please."

Ken reached up, lifted the book from her hand and placed it on the table, open at the title page. "Who should I make it out to?"

"To Frederick; that's my father. Can you add 'happy birthday'?"

Ken replied with a friendly "Sure" and began writing.

Steve picked up a book and moved back a step to make room for two people waiting behind him. He turned the pages to the preface. The first paragraphs read:

This written story—intended as a novel— originally began with a man of my age and social status describing the remarkably happy events of his life and confessing to his missteps as well.

But I sensed that the well-crafted, third person who was sorting through his sometimes poignant, sometimes joyful reminiscences would fool no one. Every reader will recognize this fellow optimistically arranging his desk at his first job, nervously renting a tuxedo for his wedding, listening quietly with moist eyes at his mother's funeral, was really Kenneth Bretsom. Therefore, I admit that the book you hold in your hand is only about me. So, it is written that way.

Steve closed the book and stuffed it under his arm, watching as the author continually grinned, shuffled some of his books, glad-handed his many admirers. He wondered if this relaxed, famous-at-the-moment scribe had spent the same restless hours as he, straining for something or someone to point out the directions for throwing the switch to bring his painfully fashioned biography to life. *How many times did he consider giving up, as I almost did?*

Steve guessed that this encounter might be providence at work. Perhaps this Mr. Bretsom, whom he had never heard of, sitting right there within arm's reach, would approve of the man who runs the show in his novel, Raymond Gearland. He will say nothing to him of what will be revealed. But there should be no harm in sharing his doubts about how to go about creating a believable figure.

The line of book buyers, pleased with their crisp, new, signed editions, moved on. Now alone with

Bretsom, Steve spoke firmly to get the author's attention. "Ken, a question."

Ken leaned forward in his chair. "Let me have it, Steve."

Steve tapped the book. "The story is in the first person. From your paragraph up front, though, I am led to think you were considering other ways to spin the story of your life."

"Yeah. I toyed with the dream of creating a memorable character that the reader bonds with immediately. The plan was to have my character endure my emotions, mouth my words, think my thoughts. But I didn't feel comfortable; It would have been different if I had been *inventing* his entire world. Hell, it's all make-believe. He's confused; he's ecstatic. I can write that stuff all day. Somehow, though, I couldn't describe how someone *else* would deal with real tragedies, like the death of his father."

"You mention your father's death?"

Ken stiffened. "Yes, it's in there, and I'm not sure I got it right."

Steve took a long breath. "I've just started writing a book based on things *I've* done, people I've known, things that happened to me. I'm going through the same struggle."

A short, dark-haired woman with a large, brown tote bag laid a copy of the book and a check on the table in front of Ken. He flipped open the cover and signed. He looked back at Steve. "How are you doing so far? What approach did you decide on.?'

"I guess I'm using the idea you tossed away. I created a character—that's me, of course. His name is Ray; he relates parts of his life to another major character in the book.

Ken pushed his chair back with a scraping noise, and stood, leaning into Steve. "Who is this other major character?

"A woman."

"Oh, really? An old, sympathetic school chum? A co-worker?"

"My main character just happens to meet a woman who wants to write a similar book about *her* life but hasn't been able to. They start sharing their memories."

"Why did you pick a woman?"

Steve turned his head, slowly, as if in deep thought. He had a story ready, but it did not include the dream, and certainly not Bernice.

"Somehow I envisioned a woman being more receptive to what my main character reveals. I couldn't imagine some other guy taking the subject seriously. From what I've been told about women—and that includes what I've learned from my wife—they are ready to exchange feelings and little stories."

"So then, you're all set."

"Not quite."

At those two words the look of interest on Ken's face deepened. "When you thought about writing this book, did the material pour out as a natural, chronological series of events? Or did you have other arrangements you considered using?"

Steve waved his arms in frustration. "I'm worried that I've forgotten the important things that changed my direction in life, worried that I'm heading off on another tack, that I'm delving into too many regrets, too much resentment."

There was a long pause while he searched for words to wrap up his anguish. In a tone of despair, he sighed, "This isn't meant to be a book of scores I'm trying to settle." He knew Ken must have guessed from his halting words that he was floundering.

"You bring up a good point," Ken said with a subdued smile. "If you should have the misfortune of writing a best seller, your reviewers won't spend too many words describing your brilliant ability to evoke striking images and profound emotions, they will start researching your life to find out—and reveal—what you did that really underlies the adventures of your characters . . ."

Ken paused his remarks as a woman's voice from an overhead speaker announced that the book signing will close in ten minutes.

When the room went silent, Ken continued his lecture, his head pivoting in exasperation, his arms flailing. "Some reviewers seemed to be compelled to find meanings in everything I write. They're just stories, Steve, painfully and laboriously concocted, but just *stories*, for chrissakes." He looked into Steve's eyes to see if he caught the message, noting he had his attention. "It's the same way with dreams. There are people to whom I can't relate an interesting dream I had without them missing the fun of it, instead pondering on some deep meaning."

That topic was too tempting. Steve couldn't resist the opportunity to ask the gnawing question in the back of his mind. "That's a good point, Ken. Have you ever used material from a dream?" That was a mistake. He tensed, expecting Ken to turn the question around and ask *him* about dreams. That could be awkward.

With an emphatic, dismissive shake of his head, Ken advertised his answer. "Stuff from a dream? Never, too weird."

Steve sighed, reaching for a change in *that* subject. "Let's go back to what you were saying earlier. I have always assumed that even a so-so review was better than none. Doesn't it at least get your name out?"

Ken began smiling again, adding, "Lemme give you an example. In one of my books I had a character, a young boy, whose father traveled a lot and was seldom home. One reviewer said the trials suffered by this child in growing up probably mirrored my being brought up by an aunt. Hell, Steve. *I wasn't raised by my aunt.* She only took care of me during the day when my mother took a three-month job at the phone company."

Steve's eyebrows went up in a show of acceptance. "If someone wants to read a few more details into the descriptions of how I made my way in this world, that's okay."

Ken expressed doubt. "Are you sure? You just told me that your main character—and that reflects on you, Steve—spends most of his time exchanging memories with this woman, right?"

"That's right."

Ken's face took on an almost evil smirk. "Guess where that will lead. Some reviewer won't come right out and accuse you of having an affair, but his appraisal in the books section of your local newspaper—read by your neighbors and family members—will be politely and discreetly worded to suggest there was another woman in your life."

Steve stiffened at the assertion. *Another woman in my life!* Need he explain that the woman was a creation of a dream, a person that doesn't exist.

Ken began waving a finger, a sign of agitation. He asked, "Does your character get involved in any politics, social issues?"

"No. Why does that matter?"

"To steer you away from another bad experience I had. My main character, a college professor, becomes infatuated with one of the more mature female students in his Sociology class. And she's attracted to him. They start meeting off-campus on the pretext of discussing diversity in the workplace. On the release of my book a long review appeared in a major newspaper—as I prayed for. But instead of complimenting me on the imaginative way I handled those little teacher-student meetings where romance sets in, the damn reviewer used most of the page space analyzing my so-called political leanings that he *alleged* were reflected in the opinions exchanged by the two characters. On top of that he cited political writers he claimed I drew upon, writers I had never heard of!"

The soft, seductive woman's voice on the speaker broke in again to state the book signing was now closed and all visitors must exit. Steve and Ken watched as the small crowd of lookers and buyers headed out the door.

Ken picked up a carton from under the table and began stacking books inside. "Yeah, the moment you go public, you will become a persona of interest."

Steve shrugged. "Maybe I *will* have to suffer that intrusion into my past. Every scene is a reality I experienced. Nothing is fabricated."

"That could get you in trouble too, my boy. Here's an example. I was in the army, stationed at Fort Sheridan in Illinois. I met a beautiful girl at the USO center in downtown Chicago. I took her out on a date on every pass I had. We'd go to the movies near where she lived and we'd stop at a cozy soda fountain to have cocoa afterward. I really went for her."

Ken stopped his story, bent to the floor to pick up the small metal easel that held one of his books, and tossed it in the carton. "I was transferred to another military base and didn't see her for most of a year. We exchanged letters weekly. When I received my discharge, Steve, my *first* trip was back to Chicago. I took the 'L' to the west side of the city to her neighborhood. As the train was reaching a station, I happened to look out the window and couldn't believe what I saw. There she was, alone on the platform, in a blazing white blouse and a contrasting dark skirt—unbelievably beautiful— waiting to get in *my* car! She did. The other passengers must have been shocked or at least puzzled why a soldier jumped up and wrapped his arms around some woman that just stepped aboard."

"That really happened?" Steve asked, eyebrows at maximum elevation.

"Yes, and I put that scene in one of my books. Get this, more than one of the copy editors at my publisher said they thought my book was intended as serious drama, not light romance. They said the episode was improbable, too phony, too story-book."

Ken finished packing. Almost glaring, he said, "The lesson here, Steve, is be judicious about how much you reveal about those affairs that you think illuminated your life, especially the inopportune ones."

Steve grunted, "That's the core of my problem. I realize all the things that were painful don't *have* to be included—mistakes I made, downturns of fate.

Still, something keeps pushing me to disgorge those messes in my life."

Ken looked down at the pile of books in the carton, straightened them carefully, and said, "I know what you're going through. I've been there. I guess your dilemma falls under the heading of artistic choice." He rubbed his forehead. "Think of it this way: who are you trying to please—the one reader that can't deal with your agony over never getting the bicycle you wanted for Christmas—or the hundred readers that smile, seeing themselves when you write about your whole class being held hostage after school to punish some unidentified kid shooting spit balls?

"Those choices are there, staring at me often," Steve said. "I wish I had someone like you, sitting next to me, to remind me of where I'm supposed to be going."

Ken, with a pinched look, wagged his head, spoke grimly. "Sorry, pal. You're all alone in this game." Then he smiled. "The only way I could give you a transfusion of smarts is to write your whole damn book—and I'm not about to offer to do that."

Steve grinned, somewhat sheepishly. "Well, let me ask the ten-dollar question: how do I get my book published."

"You need an agent."

"I know. I found that out in my novel writing class from several of the people there. But they couldn't tell me where to find one."

Ken reached into his pocket for his wallet. He retrieved it and let it fall open. He pulled out a business card. "This is the woman I use. Her name is Linda Kosolow. She works with authors and publishers who do biographies, memoirs and the like."

"How do I get started?"

"Call her; write her. She'll tell you what she needs."

"Is she around here?"

"Hell, no. She's in New York. Everything will be done by postal mail or email. How far along are you on the book?"

"I have only one chapter," Steve said, "But it's written well."

"She will ask you for a synopsis and maybe three chapters. She's good. She will tell you if there is a chance that one of her publisher contacts will pick it up or whether you're wasting your time."

Steve fingered the card, turning it carefully, studying it. He slid it into an empty slot in his wallet, then checked his bankroll. There was enough cash to pay for his copy and leave. As he tugged on one of the bills inside, a small piece of paper fell out–the note with the book title the reference desk woman had given him. He grabbed for it, but it hit the floor and rolled under the table. As he tried to scrape it back with the toe of his shoe, it disappeared, bouncing farther away. No loss. He reached into the wallet again and pulled out a twenty-dollar bill which he held up to Ken. "Will this cover the book?"

Ken raised his hand, rejecting the offer. "Forget it. Have a copy on me. You can send me a copy of yours."

Steve rested the book in the bend of his elbow. "I appreciate your encouraging me, Ken, trusting that I might have something that won't waste this Kosolow lady's time."

Ken threw his palm up lightly against Steve's shoulder. "To show your gratitude, go home and start writing."

Two elderly women, who had not yet departed the room, came up to the table and pulled books from the carton. Steve said, "It looks like you have customers waiting. I'm interrupting your business."

Ken took the books from the women and seated himself, grabbing his pen. He looked up one last time at Steve. "My contact info is in the bio at the end. Let me know how you're doing."

As Steve turned to go, two men entered the room, placed Ken's box of books on the carpet, then moved the table and chair against a wall of the room. Ken picked up the box, gasping, waved briefly to Steve as he walked out and down the hall.

Alone, staring at the empty, quiet room, Steve thought about the note again—the title for the book that the reference desk woman recommended. He looked at the carpet for the scrap of paper from his wallet. It was nowhere. Apparently one of the library workers picked it up as he set the furniture aside.

The stillness of the room made way for thoughts about where he should turn next. He had to admit, for all of the lecturing by Mrs. McFarland in the writing workshop, for all of the fatherly advice of Bretsom, and last, for all the intimate exchanges with Bernice, he was still reaching for that mode of language by which he could express himself. Dohlstram had suggested he pick and mimic an author with a style that fit his taste. Maybe, it was time for him to do a little innocent plagiarizing, time to do some actual reading. Perhaps he should start with the book Miss Wilkins, the reference desk woman, recommended. What was the name of that book? He left the room, traversed the hallway, and entered the main library, getting his bearings on the reference desk.

The walkway through the reading area and into the vast depths of the book stacks had signs on stands announcing library events. As he passed one, his vision lined up with the counter where Miss Wilkins had sat, but a small man was sitting there now, an older man. Steve approached and asked, "Is Miss Wilkins around?"

"She's left for the day. Can I help you?"

"I don't think so. She suggested a book, but I don't remember enough of the title. I'll try another time." He turned and walked toward the western exit that opened to the Anna Vail senior center.

Steve reached into his side of the closet off the master bedroom and pulled his red plaid pajamas from a hook to his right. He thought about Evelyn's pajamas that were always folded neatly each morning and placed on a small bench in the bathroom. Evelyn considered his method of storing nightwear messy, but it was quick and functional.

He undressed and donned the pajamas, tightening the drawstring on the waist. He lowered himself to the edge of the bed and picked up his notebook from where it was propped against the lamp on the nightstand. Next to it was the stub of a pencil. He grasped it and began writing,

Evelyn entered the room, noticed his uninterrupted attention to his notebook, and stepped toward him to look down at his moving hand. "More notes for your novel?"

He looked up. "Yeah, some ideas were passed along to me at the library today when I dropped off your books."

"Really?"

"There was a book signing. I stopped by, got to meet and talk to the author."

"Anybody I know?"

"His name is Ken Bretsom. His books are sort of in the line of what I'm trying to do."

"Never heard of him. Was he any help?"

Steve laughed. "As a matter of fact, he clearly refused to help me write my book, but he gave me a few tips and a good lead on getting published."

Evelyn's eyes widened. "See, aren't you glad you volunteered to make the drop-off." He ignored her and kept writing. She touched his shoulder. "Excuse me, I've got to change."

She disappeared into the bathroom and closed the door. Steve continued to make notes. When she returned many minutes later, dressed for bed, Steve had put the notebook back on the nightstand and was under the blanket, stretched out.

She backed into her side of the bed and crawled in, sitting upright against a stack of pillows. "I'm going to read awhile. Will that bother you?"

"No. I'm really tired. I think I did too much today. Besides, that wine at dinner made me sleepy."

He rolled over to his left and turned off the lamp on his nightstand. He felt fully relaxed; there were no pending tasks or problems to resolve. As each minute passed, he felt himself slipping deeper and deeper into a thoughtless state. Then some vague images crossed his vision. He awakened to the dream world.

EMERGING PATTERN

TWO young boys and their mother strolled the walk that bordered the children's play yard in Maple Bounty Park. Steve watched them enter the wooded area and get lost behind the tall bushes and tree branches. It was strangely silent. There was no movement of air, no sound or sight of birds. Something was wrong; the swings, the slide and the roundabout were unoccupied and motionless. And they were not in the designated locations. Had someone directed that they be repositioned? Why was he sent to this part of the park today, and what did they want him to check? This was Carl Firbrooke's area.

He turned his head first toward the cloudy sky, shielding his eyes from the sun with a clipboard he was holding, then toward the horizon. In the distance were some unfamiliar buildings. Where was the recreation and park district headquarters? There were more benches than he remembered being placed here when the playground was designed. What's more, they had become terribly weather-worn; now they were an eye-catching bright teal and looked brand new. He counted two sparkling, new trash containers. Who ordered these? He looked down at the clipboard. There were some sketches and symbols that didn't make sense. What was he supposed to do?

He felt a firm tap on his shoulder. He looked in the direction of the tap to see the arm of a woman. He turned quickly to confront her. It was Bernice! How long had she been there?

She was leaning against a leg of the swing set. Her white, long-sleeved, embroidered peasant blouse had vertical strings of yellow daisies that gleamed in the bright daylight. Her skirt was dark and full with an unusually distinct white floral pattern. She raised her hand slightly. "Hello, stranger."

He looked at her face; his first thought was *how distinctive*. He could pick her out of a crowd of a hundred. "My God, what are you doing here?"

"Isn't this where you hang out during the day?"

"On occasion."

She made two steps to the side, lowered herself into the belt of one of the swings, raised her legs, and swayed in the sun. "I haven't been to a playground since I was eight years old." She gave the ground below a little kick and the arc of her swing increased. She looked up at the empty sky, searching. "The swings were my favorite. My father took me to parks and lifted me onto the swings. He always pushed me really hard and I would scream."

"I could give you a good push, but I don't want to hear you scream." He reached over, gazed down at her, and playfully shook one of the lengths of chain supporting her. As he looked at her intently, features of her body he had not noticed before became apparent, features that had been covered by her jacket and jeans when she first came upon him in The Select Cup. Her neck was spare, no flab, and the skin was taut. He looked down at her calves, not too muscular, and smooth. To his surprise he was becoming attentive to how physically attractive she was.

She saw him looking; she reached down and raised her skirt. She tilted her head toward her shoes. "At least I can say my legs are still holding up."

He purposely looked away into the grove of maples, but she continued. "I think it's the tennis that keeps them in shape. I love tennis."

She slid out of the swing, stood a moment while she brushed the back of her skirt, and walked toward a bench beneath a tree.

"It's getting hot. Let's sit in the shade and talk."

He followed her. She leaned over the bench, knocked away a few leaves that had fallen from the red maple tree above, and sat down. Steve took his seat next to her. He noticed how she fell back in the bench, almost ignoring him. She was relaxed, different from the woman who, somewhat nervously, presented herself to him in the coffee shop. Why had she tracked him down? Had she cooked up some new recipe for the ingredients of his novel? She had become more authoritative. Every movement she made, every word she spoke, seemed pre-meditated. She radiated an aura of control.

Bernice looked at him for a long while before speaking. "You *know* what I'm going to ask. How is the writing going?"

He sensed concern in her question; perhaps some enthusiasm was needed. He nodded emphatically as he answered. "It's going well. Ray has been having long and frequent talks with Phyllis."

"Great. I take it, then, you found the plot arrangement workable."

"Very workable. There were so many things I wanted to say—they wouldn't come; now I'm able to. As I write about those times in my life—the ones that dart about in my head—now they seem to be more intense. It's almost as if I was reliving them."

"Did you describe our first meeting?

"In the coffee shop? Yeah. I have Ray discover Phyllis in the parking lot. She has a pickup truck with a dead battery. He invites her to join him in the shop while they wait for the road-service truck."

"*I* have a pickup. I had it custom painted—burnt orange."

He straightened, with a look of surprise. "Really? You must offer me a ride sometime."

Her voice was relaxed but held strong intent. "I plan to."

Her tone and her posture grew rigid. She asked softly, "Did you have Phyllis relate the story about the dress?"

"The dress in the store window? A little. To be truthful I devoted most of my current writing to what *Ray* was thinking about."

She looked at him sternly. "I want you to include what I told you about the pink dress; it's important to me."

"I've just started that chapter; I'll be sure to mention more about the dress."

"Do you remember the story?" she asked.

"Yes, I'm sure I got all the details right. But it needs some work," he said, realizing too late that she would pounce.

"Some work? What is that?"

"It's kind of dry. I described your love for the dress—and your disappointment. But I don't think I've made the reader feel the same way you did."

In a show of concern, she leaned toward him, her hand blocking the sun on her face. "Did my story leave *you* with some thoughts about how the little girl felt?"

"Of course; I was moved by it."

He pondered a moment on how to explain why his treatment of his and her stories lacked something, something he couldn't put his arms around. "Here's what happens, Bunny. I write words that capture the essence of those things you've told me. Then I stop, sit there, just staring at the page, reading those simple sentences over and over. They're too bland. There's got to be more to it than that."

"Certainly, there *is* more," she said. Then her lecture began. "When you're here, Steve, sitting with me, listening to me, you're also thinking about things, right?"

She brought her eyes closer to his, pointed a finger first over her shoulder, then at herself. "You're looking at things, like the clouds behind me or my rapidly moving lips, right?" She laughed. "You're doing things, like nervously clasping your hands as I talk."

"Yes."

"As trite as you think those thoughts, those visions, those movements are, Steve, put them down. Okay?"

He bowed his head a little, smiling. "Yes, mam."

Now she began smiling. The urgency she displayed earlier vanished. She tilted her head artfully. "What are some other memories you want *Ray* to bring up?"

"There are a lot, but each one connects to a different part of his life. I'd like to link each memory to the person Ray meets up with."

Bernice stiffened. "What do you mean by that?"

"Well, in the book Ray encounters other people."

"Other people?"

"Yes. I see Ray as having lived a full life. Some of his close friends have died, and I plan to have him talk about the sorrow that comes when he is told or reads about their passing. But many friends are still alive. It's natural for him to want to see them now and then—shoot the breeze."

She smiled at him, a sign of forgiveness for his foolish remark, then she said, "I understand. However, those are just off-and-on friends. His most meaningful and most lengthy talks should be with Phyllis."

"Why is that?"

"Because Phyllis finds herself bonding with Ray; she has a strong personal need to know what concerns him. His sharing of his life with her provides significance to *her* life."

He was about to object; instead he controlled his need to speak. He allowed that her argument might be valid. Phyllis *could* be the main customer of Ray's tales. Still, he might need space to in which to navigate in chapters down the road. There might be a reason to confide in someone else. After all, it *was his* novel.

Her words interrupted his internal debate. "Steve, tell me some more about yourself. Were there any, what could be called, life-changing events?"

He was on to her. She was trying to draw him out. He was beginning to wonder if she really gave a damn. Should he open himself completely to this woman he's known for only about an hour and a half. Why not? There were things that had to go in the book somewhere. Maybe this was an opportune time for Ray to tell Phyllis about his time in the Navy.

She prodded him. "Were you always as self-assured as you seem now?"

"Of course not, Bunny. I don't know how you can keep a straight face when you ask that question."

"Tell me what occurs to you."

A trove of memories of his service in the Navy that had never surfaced before suddenly presented themselves. Strange that her question should send him back to that point in time. He was surprised that he was about to recount something he had never told anyone.

"Bunny, in the last weeks before my high school graduation I reminded my dad that I wanted to go to college. I had no firm idea what I wanted to study, but I knew I wanted to have the opportunity. He was proud of me for saying that; I could tell by the look on his face."

Bernice gazed into the maple forest. "I wanted to enter college—study literature. Like a fool, I got married." Her mouth had turned down slightly as she spoke. She lifted her eyes toward him. "How did it work out for you—making it into a university?"

"My dad asked me if I had a school in mind. Then, Bunny—God help me—I said something I'm ashamed to tell you or even think about. I told him I had a college picked out and . . ." Steve choked a little. "Then I asked where the money was going to come from!" Every muscle in his face tightened as he bowed his head. "God, what let me say that?"

"Maybe the old man was ready to help. A little advice, a few dollars."

"My father took me aside and explained—with great difficulty—that he had opened a savings account at his bank. He thought that with his slightly better salary at the air base he could put a little money aside each month for my college tuition. But with mortgage and insurance payments and medical and household expenses he couldn't keep up the deposits."

He looked directly into Bernice's eyes. He wanted very much for her to feel his anguish. "It was hard for him to disappoint me, Bunny; hard for him to admit that he aimed too high. But he *did* tell me about the account; he could have kept it a secret."

"He realized you had the strength, the smarts to find a way, by yourself, to make it through college."

"How would you know that?"

She hesitated, tugging awkwardly on her sleeve.

"I think I know what kind of man your father was."

"How?"

She made small, uneasy movements in the bench. "Well, from what you've told me."

He didn't recall ever mentioning his poverty-level existence to her. Her remark evoked evening scenes where he, clad in pajamas, shuffled into the kitchen to say good night to his parents, finding them in an argument over how the bills would ever get paid. When he appeared, they would change the subject. He pretended he hadn't heard, but he wanted to tell them that he would soon grow up, get a job, and help with expenses.

Steve sighed, "I had never expected him to put money aside; I wasn't disappointed in the least."

"So, what did you do?"

"I joined the Navy."

"You became a sailor. I can just visualize you in your uniform."

He patted his hips. "I have one pair of pants—and a jumper maybe—put away somewhere. They don't fit me anymore."

"Was the duty stressful?"

"Once I received my rating, there was no stress; it was just a job. Boot camp was an adjustment though."

"Were they tough on you?"

"Not really. It was just the leaving home. There I was, an unworldly teenager accustomed to sleeping in my own soft bed in a room near my parents. All of sudden I'm in a hard mattress in a barracks with dozens of guys like me, strangers, lying in their bunks down the line. Now I'm washing my own clothes, keeping the barracks scrupulously clean, marching and exercising in the morning before chow, standing four-hour watches in the middle of the night."

Bernice placed her right hand on his arm for his attention; it felt good. "See, you've come up with more material for Ray to talk about."

He looked down, noticing her legs again as he spoke. "I've already put a reminder in my notebook to include some of my service experience. But my time in the Navy is not a simple event to recall. It was a complicated period in my life."

"*Make* it simple. You can sort through the incidents that are sticking in your head and pick out something funny or exciting that's easy to explain."

He nodded slightly to end the discussion. She made it sound so easy.

She made a writing gesture with her finger. "Got your notepad?

"Why?

"I should tell you another of *my* stories."

"Go ahead; I'll remember."

"What kind of a story would you like to hear?"

"A happy story, preferably," he said.

As she began to speak, he raised his hand to interrupt. "Actually, I want you to dig way back to your earliest memory. Can you do that?"

Her head snapped up as if she were caught off-guard. She lowered her eyes and covered them with her palm. "There *is* one. It's not pleasant." She gave him an apologetic look. "But it turned out okay. Do you really want to know?"

He hesitated. He could see she was not eager to reveal what crossed her mind. But he had asked and he couldn't back down. "Yes, I do. What happened?"

She began gripping the edge of the bench by her knees very firmly as she spoke quietly. "For the memory to make sense I have to explain. One evening I mentioned to my father there had been a discussion about serious communicable diseases in my high school class. He surprised me; he told me that when I was about eighteen months old, I had contracted diphtheria. It was serious. There was no medicine for treating it. Half of the people who caught it died. It was very infectious."

The fact of Bernice's presence—there in front of him—raised a dozen questions in Steve's mind, but he made only one comment. "Somehow you survived."

"Doctors in those days made house calls. Our family doctor had me moved *immediately* to a separate room in the house and they kept the door closed. My father and mother were not allowed in. My father was able to find a nurse—I guess she had recovered from the disease herself—who took care of me. She fed me, bathed me, gave me pills. I don't remember any of that part."

"Maybe it's better you don't."

"But this is what I *do* remember. I guess it was on a morning that my condition and symptoms convinced the doctor I had recovered. I clearly see myself walking around the little room—my prison cell—in the morning while my nurse sat in a chair watching me. I remember seeing my mother and father standing outside the house, looking through the closed window at me, smiling bravely, waving excitedly. I think the nurse told me that I was going to be all right and that she would be leaving. I must have grown to love her; I remember running to her and throwing my arms around her legs and crying for her to stay."

"That's remarkable."

"Steve, for years I never knew what that memory meant. It didn't make sense until my mother explained everything. I asked her one day when we were alone why my father had never said anything about my treatment for diphtheria at home. She was surprised that he even mentioned my getting the disease. 'He could barely handle it,' mom said. Then she put her arms around me and cried. 'He told me never to bring it up. We thought we had lost you.' We cried together."

After Bernice finished her story, she became very quiet. She first looked down at the multi-colored gravel at the foot of the bench, then back to Steve. She reached over and took his two hands in hers. Her words seemed to come with difficulty. "Steve, you are the only person I've ever told that story to." Her fingers pressed his. The pleading of her eyes matched her voice. "I'm asking you from my heart. Please, please add that to your book."

He had no choice but to consent. "I will, Bunny. I think I've got it right."

She continued to watch him, silently.

As he felt the touch of her hands on his, he noticed the contraction of a muscle in his left ankle that grew into an intense pain. He tried to disregard it, but it became overwhelming. He bent over, stretching his arm to his leg to touch it.

He became suddenly aware he was in his bed attempting to extract his leg from the bedsheet. The tendons in his foot tightened even more painfully, pulling his toes up. He threw the covers back and reached down to rub his foot.

Evelyn rolled over toward him. "What's wrong? Another cramp?"

He grunted, "A bad one."

"Get up and walk around a little. That'll help."

He swung his legs down and stood. "I'll be okay."

The pain subsided slightly. He sat on the edge of the bed, scratching his head, loosening his pajama top. He said again, "I'll be okay."

Evelyn turned away and lowered her head to her pillow. She became very still. Steve began to think back to the last moments of the dream. *God, it was real!*

He thought he should take the advice of the good doctor Dohlstram—write down the dream events before they faded. Would they ever? That wasn't happening. The details of the encounter with Bernice that ended only moments ago seemed exceptionally vibrant. What was the last of his topics to cover she urged him to tackle? Oh, yeah, the thrill of the Navy.

Next to him on the nightstand was his notebook. He picked it up and walked from the bedroom to the den where he pressed the white button on the small lamp. The fluorescent tube flickered, then flooded the area with a soft light. He pulled the chair back from the desk and collapsed into it, the notebook on his lap unfolded at a bookmark he had inserted.

He waited until the cramp in his foot had run its course. Then he looked down at the open pages, picked up a worn pencil from the desk and touched it to the paper on which he had scrawled "sea stories."

He addressed himself dramatically, "Well, Mr. Ribman, what have you to say about life in the ny-vee?", mouthing the word with what he considered an accent. Those two words recalled one night—an almost unendurable night—in boot camp at the Naval base.

The image he brought up was very distinct. Posted on the barracks watch list one morning was his name and watch assignment—his first: "Ribman, K Barracks, Morning Watch"—the four a.m. to eight a.m. on the following day.

Uncertain as to whether he could survive with four hours of lost sleep, he had hit the sack early that night—a bit futile in the presence of the surrounding banter from his "shipmates" playing cards and describing life in their home states. Keith DeLonge was particularly noisy when a good hand came around.

He had anticipated the early wake-up call, but he couldn't believe that more than a few minutes had passed since his head hit the pillow. His slumber was deep. The hand of the young man standing the middle watch in their barracks shook his shoulder roughly. "Time to get up, sailor," he announced.

He slid out of bed, almost landing on the floor, quietly donned the clothing he had placed at the ready under his bunk, pulled his knitted cap over his stubby-haired head, and wobbled, somewhat sleepy, out the door.

Outside he stopped, straightened his jumper, and inhaled a deep sample of the cool night air. The grounds and sidewalks of the entire base surrounding him were dark and abandoned. As he looked at the row of barracks receding far into the shadows, a massive uncertainty arose, a tremor stirred his chest; The realization dawned that he had no idea as to where he was to go. Which building was Barracks K? He would have to do some exploring.

Down the walk that bordered the drill field he paused at each building, looking for some designation; they were all alike. There was not a person to ask where K barracks was. The area was poorly lit, but then who would be out at this time of night other than a boot like him heading for his watch station?

Yesterday morning he should have had someone point out that particular barracks while they were outside exercising on the grinder—the parade ground—swinging their M1903 Springfield rifles over their heads to the tempo of the martial music that blared from the speaker on the platform, high above their heads, where a second class petty officer, sweeping the sky with his own rifle, led them in their bends and stretches.

His hopes were raised when he noticed a dull glint from a framed sign next to each barracks doorway. He stepped up to one to get a closer look. It was too dark to fully read, but the letter "K" was visible. His anxiety vanished. He went inside.

The building was deserted, lined with long rows of empty bunks. Something seemed wrong. Shouldn't there have been a midwatch waiting to be relieved?

He shouted, "Morning watch arriving! Anybody here?" No answer came. He stood still in the silent darkness, listening only to his own breath. Why was he here? Why would they set a watch in an unused barracks? But then, this was probably part of the training. Perhaps this was meant to prepare him for the monotony of standing a watch at sea when there wasn't another ship within two hundred miles.

He stood just inside the entry, looking out of the small panes in the front door. There was little to see. Across the grinder and a patch of lawn was the Administration Building, fronted by a naked flagpole.

The clouds had moved away from the moon; the empty landscape became reasonably visible. If an attacking Navy from an enemy country were to attempt a maneuver into the base, he could easily identify them. There had been a warship recognition class two days ago conducted by Chief Petty Officer Beale. Steve had misidentified two enemy craft, but he did okay overall. On the other hand, if he did see something suspicious, who was he to notify?

Fifteen minutes passed; he was feeling tired already. Maybe a change of scene would overcome the fatigue. He moved, one small step at a time, keeping his hands on the walls and grabbing the barely visible bunk frames as he found his way to the rear door. He opened it and surveyed the yard in back. It was, of course, without any signs of activity.

Further beyond were the clotheslines of the other barracks. Hanging from the lines were a variety of belongings: pillow cases, mattress covers, shorts, T shirts. They fluttered like white flags reflecting the moonlight. He knew that each item was securely tied with a short piece of cord—a clothes stop. The Navy didn't issue clothespins.

The lack of any activity to occupy his attention was a sign this would be a long night. Standing in one place for more than a few minutes was something he had never done in his eighteen years. It was boring and uncomfortable. He braced himself on the door frame then looked back into the darkness of the barracks for a chair to sit on; there were none. He could sit on the floor, but he might end up asleep. In fact, if he remembered right, he was to "stand" his watch, not sit. Besides, the Master-at-Arms might be showing up any minute to confirm he was there doing his duty.

He hadn't written his mother for a week. The short notes she sent to him came every few days all saying the same thing: she and my father were "fine", and she was worried because she hadn't heard from him. There were at least two letters he had started that were crumpled and tossed away. The words about his loneliness were true but not suitable for his mother. How could he describe his sense of inferiority to some of the other men? There was this constant fear that he might not be up to some of the training. How to explain that? What he always wrote in return was more of an excuse. He reassured his mother in his sloppy handwriting that if he were ill, he would have more time to write, but he was healthy and very busy.

I promise to write, Mom. He reached up and touched the breast pocket in his jumper; it was empty. If he had a pencil and could find some paper, he could write about the watch he was on—if he could see what he was writing.

As he looked again out the door at the shadowy shapes of the laundry lines and surrounding buildings, he thought about the hundreds of men asleep at that moment—except in the barracks he now guarded. How he wished he were one of them. He breathed shallowly then deeply; trying to think of something to relieve the boredom. He shifted his weight first to one leg then the other. Something to eat would be nice. Should he have smuggled in a candy bar? A cup of hot coffee would be better.

His head became heavier. He looked down at the floor and at the gleaming toes of his shoes. He had shined them recently before the last inspection.

He knew the time was passing, but painfully slow. The same questions kept returning. Were his father, mother, and sister all right—really? What training will there be today after dawn breaks and the watch ends? Will he be up to it?

How he wished he were home. When he signed up, he was at first apprehensive about the rigors of boot camp, but the strict discipline was not a problem. His father was right. He had said, "Steve, they will just want to see if you can follow orders. Do that, and you won't have any trouble."

Something appeared in the distant shadowy area that startled him. In the space among the clothes lines where the large white fabrics were flapping, a figure appeared, then it moved back into the night, out of sight. It looked like a man dressed in black. He watched the spot intently. It was vacant; the figure was gone. Was it just the light playing tricks?

He kept watching. It didn't make sense. Why would someone be out hanging laundry after midnight? There was a tightness in his chest. He began to sway to the left and right, paying attention to every item that moved. There was nothing. He was getting very tired.

He closed the door, turned back into the entry, and leaned against the wall for support. Curiosity about the mysterious figure continued to occupy his thoughts. He felt he should look again, but he hesitated. This was foolish; there was no reason for anyone to be out there. But the image he had seen persisted. He had to confirm his suspicions. He swung the door open and watched a mattress cover tossing about as though it had a life of its own. There. . . was. . . something. . . there. He was sure it was the shoulder and arm of someone. Then it was gone again.

It may have been nothing; but was it nothing? Was this a test? He was always open to the dismal rumors that circulated in the barracks, but there were no rumors about setups being used to see if the watches were alert. In a whisper he began reciting to himself the eleventh general order of a sentry that he had carefully learned: "To be especially watchful at night and during the time for challenging, to challenge all persons on or near my post, and to allow no one to pass without proper authority."

How could he challenge that distant, fleeting image anyway? He was not sure he should leave his station and walk across the yard to confront whatever it was that was playing hide and seek among the pillow cases blowing in the night breeze.

There were thoughts about his sister, Alice. What was she doing? She had not written him yet; maybe she never would. He had not written to her. What could he say?

Now that he was far away from the sound of her voice and her movement in their home, he realized how little he knew of her interests and friends. She was a little older and had connections he didn't. She hung around with some racing car drivers. How in Hell did she meet them?

It seemed like the dawn would never come, but a gray light rose in the East making the buildings more recognizable. He opened the door and looked out at the clothes lines where the intruder had been playing hide and seek. Everything was visible: the forest of poles, the crisscross of clothes lines, and the endless array of white rectangles of cloth, like surrender flags. There was no person there.

As Steve closed the notebook, he wondered if he was capable of committing that vague episode to paper. He carefully positioned his fingers on the keyboard and began typing. A paragraph came very quickly. He pulled his hands back, placed them in his lap and stared at what he had written.

An awareness had grown in him that when he was not distracted, when he was quiet for a while, words—whole sentences—were appearing that he hadn't planned. It was though someone else was doing the writing. It was also at times like this that his mind opened to an increasing scope of material that might be tapped. In fact, it was unnerving. He was getting glimpses of a frightening, large panorama of a young Steven Ribman doing things he had dismissed before. There he was, at the age of ten, sitting atop the handlebars of Ralph's bicycle, yelling with outrageous joy, while Ralph did all the hard pedaling. These were treasured moments that called out to be given their place in his book.

He found the memories were now exerting power over him; they were demanding to be brought back to life. The words that described them had to be chosen very, very carefully. It was important, not only to project a crystal sharp image, but he must, somehow, evoke in the reader the laughter or the tremor that he had felt. He found himself being drawn in to more and more re-creations of his past. That was good and that was bad. There were days in his life he never wanted to live again.

But *he* was in charge of how the story would be told; *he* was the one to choose those events that would be inserted, and *he* would set the tone of their description. That is precisely how he will proceed at that moment and in the days to come. The irrefutable logic of his approach filled him with resolve and energized his fingers. Words were now filling the page.

GRAVE MOMENTS

WITH two full days of productive writing under his belt, using material forged from his Sunday dream, Steve began thinking back to those milestones in his life that had hounded him into starting his project, memories he had passed over in his rush to get his dialogue with Bernice on paper.

He flipped open his notebook near the first entries to see which thoughts had taken priority when he first toyed with the prospect of a novel. Each page had lines of random words, complete sentences, and occasional paragraphs neatly separated. These were the keys to unlock the memories that often came and went. There was one entry that simply said: *1989-The last phone call.* He was surprised that it had occurred to him, that he had included it. It was a reference to a memory that he had never revealed to anyone, not to Evelyn, and never to his sister.

About a month before Alice's disturbing, late-night report to him about his father's heart attack, the old trooper had called him. On one weekend evening while he was in the garage checking the faucets in the deep sink, the phone on the wall next to the furnace buzzed. When he picked up the handset, he recognized his father's voice; His words were, as always, "This is your dad calling." Hearing from him was not unusual. His father would ring him up occasionally to exchange stories about the local weather, recent purchases at the supermarket, ironic events at the local restaurant, any excuse to call.

But his father didn't have the usual tidbit to share. His voice was a little unsteady. "You know, Steve, we've had a good life together. Don't you agree?"

Steve was startled. That choice of words was out of place and disquieting. "We sure have, dad. I can't complain."

His father's words came slowly. "We got to do a lot together. Remember the time we rented the boat and went fishing? That was the first and only time. You caught a big one. Do you remember?"

"I was pretty young. I can't recall the fish. I think it was a yellow perch. I remember I stuck the hook in my finger. That hurt, but you got it out."

"You were a good son. You studied hard and made something of yourself. I was always proud of you."

"I tried to be, dad. You set a good example for me and Alice."

The tone of the discussion was troubling. He felt his reaction should be to stay positive. Probably his father had fallen into a sentimental mood and needed to talk.

His father's voice came again, hesitant and broken. "Yeah, we had some great times. You could write a book about those times, Steve. If you do, be sure to mention me. Tell how we were pals. Of course, mention your mother as well. She used to take you everywhere when I was out of town. I'll always regret how my overtime at the airbase kept you and me from a lot of ball games. But that's what you have to do to put the meat on the table."

The thought occurred that his father was now suffering bits of guilt, as Steve now was, unbearable guilt for not grasping those precious moments when they stood, man to man, father and son, and failed to reach out to even clasp a hand on an arm or look at each other in the eye.

Steve could barely control the emotion that was arising in his voice. "I've never thought about those times you weren't at home, dad; I never felt neglected. But you're right; that's what you had to do." He was growing uncomfortable. "What prompted you to bring that up on our special weekly phone call?"

There was a long pause. Steve wondered if he had lost the connection. He heard his father clear his throat. "I'm calling, Steve, to let you know I'm really lacking in the health department. I'm really old, my boy. I'm amazed I've lived this long."

"I'm grateful you have, dad."

"I hate to trouble, you, Steve, with bad news, but I feel I'm really at the end."

At that very second, as the last phrase echoed in his ear, he knew why his father had called. How to respond? He couldn't find the words for what he was really thinking, but something had to be said. He found himself mouthing an empty assurance he must have prepared for this moment. "Hey, you've been old for a long time, dad. You've got a while to go." Was that believable? What else could he say that wasn't trite? He had to lift his father's spirits. "There are still a lot of good times ahead . . ."

His father interrupted. "With your mother gone, I have no one to worry about, thank God.

Although it's terribly lonely. There's no way I can get around by myself to do anything. I'm sick of just sitting, sitting. Your sister comes over a lot to help out. I don't know what I would do without her. But she shouldn't have to do that, Steve. She's got her own life to live."

Words in answer came to Steve's mind, but they were meaningless. He stammered, "Dad, if there is something . . ."

But his father wasn't listening. "I keep looking for reasons to keep living. I'm tired, Steve. I'm tired of worrying if the electric bill got paid. Tired of making decisions, like how much damn fire insurance for the house. I don't have the energy. I can't deal with things anymore. I'll miss my music, Steve. You know how I loved my songs." The line went silent again.

His father's voice, harboring overpowering stress, was not recognizable. It was the voice of a man trying very hard to speak in calm and matter-of-fact tones, but anger and fear were modulating that voice now that the end was coming at a time not of his choosing. In Steve's entire life, he had never heard his father express anguish over any of the dozens of adversities that always arose. At least he never complained in front of his children. When there was bad news, his father might raise his eyebrows as if surprised, maybe even smile; then he would shrug it off with a philosophical remark. He never let on that it was something tough to handle, perhaps wanting to shield his children from the suffering of problems that were his alone.

Arthur began speaking again. "This is hard to say, Steve, but I'm not going to be around much longer. I wanted you to know how much I have loved you as a son."

How could he respond to that? His throat had tightened to the point he couldn't speak. He couldn't take a deep breath and utter words at the same time. "It's more than I can bear to hear you say that, dad, but I thank you for telling me. I know it is not easy for you to do this."

His father's tone lightened; becoming almost artificially jovial. "I've got to hang up now, Steve. Got some of that damn medicine waiting for me, you know. I really hate taking all that crap."

"Okay, dad. Please call again. Soon."

He thought he heard a click. The line went dead. He carefully replaced the handset. He needed to go somewhere in the house where he could sit, be alone, and be quiet. He remembered heading for the den. It was dark and empty there. He had let himself fall splayed into the swivel chair, his mind numb and in disbelief of what he had heard. That was the last call from his father. A memory that couldn't be erased.

He shut the notebook. With his elbow on the arm of the chair, he closed his eyes, turned his head downward, and pressed his hand hard against his forehead. God, how he missed his father! His eyes became moist; he ran his fingertips over the lids, the tears washed into his cheeks. *Dad, I wish you could be here for five minutes.* If his father could appear in the chair next to him, he would reach over and touch his hand, feel the warm skin. He would look at him, straight on, and ask forgiveness for never using the opportunities to talk son-to-father. *I had a lot of questions for you, dad.* He knew a patient smile would appear below his father's gray, sparse moustache.

He swallowed, noticing his mouth was dry. There was a cold beer waiting for him in the refrigerator. He lifted his body, drained of life, and walked in the direction of the kitchen.

As he passed the living room, he saw Evelyn seated in her favorite well-padded, maroon armchair in front of the television set. He walked in and stood behind her. She didn't ask who was on the phone; apparently, she didn't hear the ring. That was merciful; he couldn't have handled the retelling.

On the screen a choir of young men in white robes were singing. Evelyn had turned the sound off. As he bent over her shoulder to look, she turned, startled, and punched the remote. The television screen turned black.

"What was that," he asked.

"The funeral service for that Governor What's-His-Name, the one down south that died last week.

He squeezed her shoulder. "I'm sorry. I didn't mean to interrupt the program. I spoiled it for you."

"No, you didn't. It's all a lot of the same stuff. I'm going to watch the motorcade to the cemetery."

"Was he that important?"

"I guess so, a lot of people are coming in, being interviewed, telling how admirable he was."

As Evelyn held out the remote and fingered the buttons, the image returned to the screen. Cars in a long procession were making their way under a dark, cloudy sky along a narrow road rimmed with trees.

Steve's memory of the telephone call, enlarged by the solemn proceedings he watched on the screen, brought him back again to his father's death. There was no motorcade when Arthur Ribman stopped living. Only a few family members stood next to a casket. No words, only silence, only grief, only tears on each face. Steve had felt tears like those twice before: the day he fell and bloodied his knee when he was five, and when his mother died. Yes, there should have been a motorcade for Mr. Ribman.

The slow movement of the line of cars on the television screen changed to stop-and-go as each vehicle turned, slowed, and passed through the tall, wrought-iron gate of the cemetery.

Steve nervously brushed the headrest of Evelyn's chair, his eyes fixed on the screen, reacting to the weighty composition of the black gate and the array of stone shapes beyond. He began seeing more: the figures of his father and mother looking down at a grave. Why of all nights were circumstances conspiring to resurrect unpleasant memories? He was beginning to feel like some Shakespearean character whose daily joy or sorrow is at the sadistic whim of fate.

He made a decision. "Ev," He uttered, then paused for her head to turn up.

She asked, "What is it?"

He drew himself up and spoke in a tone as straight forward as the announcement of a train departure. "I'm going to the cemetery tomorrow."

"Let me guess why." She must have sensed that the funeral they were watching preyed on his mind. She reached up and patted his hand. "It's a long drive."

The decision put his mind at ease. He made his way slowly to the kitchen where the beer in the refrigerator was waiting.

On the following day, as he entered the business office of the Quiet Forest cemetery, Steve noticed very little human activity. Set back from the entrance, a very young woman seated at the reception desk, facing her computer monitor, raised her eyes to him. Her face was dominated by her tortoise shell framed glasses. Her blouse had swirls of yellow and orange. "How may I help you?" she asked.

Steve tossed a slip of paper over the counter that landed on the keyboard. "I'm looking for this gravesite. You might find two identical names, but the one I'm looking for should say 'Junior'."

She picked up the note and began typing. She leaned into the monitor to inspect the new numbers on her screen. "Yes, I see two listings for Arthur Ribman. The same family, correct?"

He nodded affirmatively. "Did you find the 'Junior'?"

"Yes," She said, frowning slightly. "That's strange. Families are usually together."

"We couldn't arrange that. The burials were too many years apart. When my father died, all of the plots near my brother had been taken. My mother, Julianna, is here also."

"Yes, I see. Arthur Ribman, Junior is in section C, one of our older sections. You're lucky; it's in walking distance. Do you want the map for Ribman, Senior?"

"No, I know where that is."

The woman reached over to a stack and pulled out a single sheet. "This is a section map for C." She made a circle on the map. "Take this with you. I marked the grave."

"I have one more request. I believe one of my coworkers has a site here. Could you look up John Lundery?"

"Is that L, U, N, D, E, R, Y?"

"Yes."

She punched six keys. "Here it is." She pulled a sheet from a different stack, drew a pencil line around one of the little oblong figures, and handed it to Steve. He tapped the paper. "It's labeled section H, that's to the west?"

"Yes. There will be some signposts."

He folded the paper and stuffed it in his breast pocket. As he turned and moved away to the entrance, a young man about to step inside held the door for him. Did he look that old? He thanked him as he moved briskly out into the autumn air. A narrow road awaited in the distance that would take him to a long-postponed reunion.

He stood at the edge of the grave he had seen only once before in his life. The soil had scattered patches of withered grass. It was otherwise bare of vegetation. The small, glossy gray, rectangular headstone was flush with the earth. At the top was a slightly raised figure of a cherub. In small, carved letters it read "Arthur Ribman, Jr., 1927 – 1929."

His father and mother had taken him and Alice here when they were very young. What first caught his attention when they reached the site was the small, almost lifeless, rose bush that marked the center of the grave. His father had brought a bottle of water that he poured on the soil next to the stem. Steve thought, *who will water it next week*? He watched his mother take a heavy breath and run her fingers over some tears that sat beneath her eyes.

Alice was wearing one of her Sunday dresses, the blue one. She held her father's hand and twisted nervously from side to side, looking up at her father, waiting for him to say something. But he remained silent. Steve wondered what thoughts were going through his parent's minds. He had never been told the full story about the short life Junior had been dealt. He had learned about his brother by accident only a month before when he found his mother sorting the baby items in the closet.

Little Alice could not grasp the significance of the grave and did not know the story of who was in it until that moment. She was told it was her older brother, whom she had never known—a brother that had died before she was born.

His father remained silent. Steve wondered as he stood there—and again throughout his life—how his father took the loss of his first child. Did he accept it as part of the fragility of life? Did he host a bitterness and sorrow that was relieved only at his own death?

Steve and Alice were never asked to visit the cemetery again. Perhaps his father and mother went on their own. He never knew.

Steve reached down and touched the headstone. "Gotta go, little brother."

Steve stood erect, took a breath, facing the area in the distance where his father was buried. That tiny piece of land in this huge cemetery was, a few hours ago, the main objective of the long trip, but he could not bring himself to visit there. He looked to the West. He had one more stop to make.

A slender, twisting, paved path led from the grave of Arthur junior to the section marked on the paper the young woman had given him. The walk through the trees and among the small and large slabs was long, but shorter than the map suggested.

Ahead, the bent frame of an elderly man caught his eye. The man was standing near the area he sought. The wind was directing the movement of the smaller branches of the trees, shaking clusters of leaves that reflected the golden afternoon light.

He found the grave on the map. The headstone was upright and prominent. A blue, marble-like tablet protruded from the dull gray concrete base with the name JOHN LUNDERY carved in large, white raised characters.

He looked down at the strip of ground beneath the marker, knowing it covered the remains of someone that had destroyed a little bit of his life each day.

He heard steps; his gaze moved upward to find the old man he had seen earlier standing next to him. The man, his face pale and wrinkled, smiled, keeping silent. Steve's awareness was drawn to the man's dark, well-tailored suit, expensive-looking shirt, and gleaming yellow silk necktie, a study in contrasts. He asked the man, "Are you here for a funeral?"

The man smiled again, weakly. "No, I'm here to visit my wife." His arm swung out, indicating a group of graves to his right. "Her funeral was five years ago."

The man looked down to where his hand rubbed his jacket then back up at Steve. "You're probably wondering why I'm so dressed up just to traipse around the backwoods." His brows were white and bushy, his face sharply wrinkled, his mouth opened as he laughed. "Ruth, my wife, helped me pick out this suit. She loved to see me wear it. I always put it on when I come to see her. I know she'd want me to."

Steve had images of this man living alone now, cooking for himself, probably making his bed each morning the same way his wife would have wanted it. A sobering cognition caught him: how will he survive if Ev were to go? He could feel the man's loneliness, his pain, as if it had been mysteriously shared with him. He replied, softly, "Yes, she would have felt good knowing you will always visit in that suit; keep doing it"

The man responded, almost joyously, "It's the same with this bright tie; it doesn't go. But she picked it out for me. I always wore it a lot for her."

The man inspected the grave Steve stood watch over. He said in almost a whisper, "I guess you're here to pay your respects as well. . . family?"

"No, just someone I knew a long time ago."

The man gave Steve a knowing nod as if he understood. "Well, I've got to go now. Maybe we'll meet here again."

Steve raised his hand, as if saluting. "Take care. I'm hoping we can."

The man trudged down the long path to a distant parking lot, putting two crows to flight.

Steve looked once more at the name on the headstone, reaching over to feel the texture of the slab, wondering if the man resting beneath it, who had an opinion for everything, would have approved the choice.

The workplace came to mind again. He remembered how, each day, John Lundery would stride through the office area, past the cubicles, into his own sanctuary, always aloof, never looking to the right nor left. Yet, Steve discovered, he was always taking note as he walked. Did Lundery ever wonder how the staff felt or didn't he care?

He thought about that awful day, close to quitting time, when he looked up from his desk to see Lundery hovering over him, a particularly strange presence, since Lundery never made the long walk through the maze of cubicles to him with questions or orders; he was always summoned to Lundery's cave in another part of the building.

John had looked down at him, speaking in a reserved tone, implying great significance to his announcement. "I want to make you aware of something I noticed, Steve. Yesterday, when I passed the desk of your new administrative assistant, she was taking a small book from the drawer. When she saw me watching her, she appeared nervous and hurriedly threw the book back in the drawer. This has happened more than once."

Steve had difficulty envisioning the activity being talked about. He couldn't believe he was having this conversation. "You mean Janice?"

Lundery continued. "Yes, her behavior looks suspicious." With that, he wheeled about and left the office.

He had heard clearly what Lundery had said, but he couldn't make sense of it. A book? He's bothered by a book?

After Lundery was out of sight, he jumped from his chair and placed his head gently against the door frame to check his admin's station. She was gone. At her request he had allowed her to leave an hour early for a doctor's appointment. Obviously Lundery used this opportunity to issue his complaint without being noticed.

He felt angry, incapacitated, being caught up in this madness. Stepping through the doorway, he looked down at the drawers in Janice's desk, tempted to pull each one open slowly to determine the nature of this "book" that caught the great man's attention. Perhaps Lundery thought she was a sorceress and was referring to some manual of spells. He shook off the notion of even touching the drawer handle. What was he thinking? Her possessions were sacred. He would, somehow, ask Janice tomorrow to explain.

He returned to his chair at the desk, clenching his jaw muscles. He thought about Janice, about the day he had interviewed her for the position of his administrative assistant, praying to find someone as dedicated and resourceful as Irma, the last one, who ended what he had believed to be an eternal working arrangement when she quit to move with her husband to another state. "We finally found the house we were dreaming of," she had said.

On the afternoon of the interview of her replacement, Janice sat in the visitor chair in front of his desk, her hands folded in her lap, very calm, very confident. She was young, with short, brushed blonde hair, a smooth, innocent face, a filled-out but not fat body.

He looked down at the very brief resumé that the personnel department had sent him. She was fresh out of school. His first question was "Why do you think you are qualified for this position?"

Straightening herself in her chair, she spoke up immediately. "I have taken advanced secretarial training. Being very good at a position like this is my goal in life; I know I can handle the work." She pointed to her resumé lying on the desk. "As you can see, my scores in typing and shorthand are very high."

Steve had to chuckle. "Yes, they are. I hope you won't be disappointed when I tell you this. Personnel does require applicants for this job to be able to take dictation, but nobody here ever dictates letters."

After he had asked all of his questions and answered all of hers, he rose and extended his hand. "I truly appreciate your coming for this interview, Janice. We have several candidates to consider. The personnel department will notify you in about two days of our decision." She thanked him and left. As he watched her move out of sight, he had made up his mind. She will work out.

On her first day at the district office, a Monday, after she had settled in and learned where the break room was, she walked into his office and asked, "Would you like a cup of coffee?"

He was stunned for a moment. Irma, with all her wondrous qualities, had never asked him that question. Maybe delivering coffee was against her principles. He replied, "That will be outstanding—but on one condition.

"What's that?"

"On Monday, *you* buy and deliver. On Tuesday, *I* buy and bring it—for us both. We alternate each day. Friday, we do our own."

She grinned, nodding, eyes rolling. "That will be a super arrangement." She nodded again, silently, and raced away.

In the days and weeks that followed, she lived up to his expectations: always on time, her focus was on her job, letters of correspondence were perfect, her desk was impeccable.

The day following Lundery's complaint, when Steve entered the office area, Janice was already busy at her desk, studying an envelope intently, unaware of his arrival. He rapped softly on the wood. She looked up at him. "Janice," he said. "I know this sounds crazy, but do you have a special little book you keep in your desk?"

She hesitated a moment, then mumbled, "Yes." She pulled out a drawer to her right and plucked out a very small, thin book, with a dark suede cover and gold lettering. "Here it is." She showed it to Steve.

Steve explained, "Don't take this wrong, but John Lundery noticed you reading it and you seemed to be hiding it."

She looked up at Steve with sorrowful eyes. "I know. When he saw me with the book, I was afraid he would think I was reading some kind of romance novel here at work. I quickly put it back."

In a reassuring voice, Steve said, "I know you wouldn't do anything that would take time from your work."

She waved the little book again. "I check my horoscope each day."

Steve took the book from her hand, placing it at the front of her desk between a cup of pencils and the metal in-and-out trays. He said, "I want you to keep it right here in full view where you can find it and look at it anytime you want. You don't have to hide it."

She had smiled broadly. "If that's okay, I will." Her enthusiasm had set the tone for the days and weeks that followed.

Steve watched the fallen leaves tumble in the breeze across the graves, some barren, some with flags, many decorated with small pails of flowers, fresh, faded, and artificial. He looked again at the name on the stone. More was coming back.

There had been another incident prior to Lundery's casting of doubt on Janice, also fueled by his complex for occasionally micro-managing the workforce. That was the emergence of his misgivings about Mel Grofter, Steve's lead planner.

When he announced his decision to hire Mel, John threw cold water on his choice. "This guy has very little recreation and park experience," he said, with a sour expression.

Steve braved an answer. "He demonstrated to me he has excellent and provable skills in charting the budgets and workloads for competing activities. And he had excellent references; I checked them out."

John leaned back, still frowning. "He has very limited experience in areas where we may need help in the future, where we could reassign him."

"John, I can't worry about the future. I have a serious backlog of renovation and construction projects. I need some qualified help, *now*! I'm convinced he can handle them."

John leaned heavily into his desk, looking away, indicating the issue was closed. He grunted, "We'll see."

A month later, when Steve was walking near John's office, he was waved in. Steve stopped abruptly and stepped inside.

John said, as if in passing, "You may consider it a minor thing, but this morning when I passed your planner, Grofter, he was sitting back in his chair, sleeping."

Steve, unfortunately, let his show of disbelief become very visible, a mistake, knowing as he spoke that Lundery didn't want his judgements questioned. "Sleeping?"

"Well, I can't *prove* he was sleeping but he had his eyes closed. Looks bad for the office, Steve."

His instinct to question Lundery for more evidence was foremost in his mind; instead he recognized the futility of reaching for a rational explanation. He said through partially gritted teeth, "I'll check that out." He left, a tightness growing in his chest.

He walked to the office area. Everyone was busy, some on phones, some in discussions. He stood motionless near a wall, trying to phrase a question in his mind to ask Mel. He looked at Mel's cubicle.

Mel was poring through a stack of ledgers, making notes. Fortunately, the area was deserted. Their conversation wouldn't be heard. Steve approached and assumed a nonchalant stand next to him.

Mel turned up from the books. "Are you taking a breather or here to give me a new assignment?"

Steve replied grimly, "You won't believe this."

Mel was expressionless as he talked. "I've witnessed many unbelievable practices in the few weeks I've been here. One more won't surprise me."

"Someone commented to management that you were sitting here, at your desk, very laid back, with your eyes closed. The impression was that you were sleeping."

Mel didn't display any anger or contrition. "Yes, I was sort of slumped in my chair with my eyes closed. I've done that before."

"Well, someone commented."

"Yes, and I'm sure I know who that someone is."

"I'd rather not say."

"You're a fair person, Steve. Isn't it possible that I just *might* be spending a few moments that way as a means of doing my job?"

"Of course."

"Do you suppose that anonymous someone could accept that I think better that way?"

Steve's spoke some words quietly, almost to himself. "After all my years here, I still haven't figured out how some of these people reach decisions."

Mel sniffed, "That whine you're telling me about is probably just a sample of crap you have to put up with. It won't happen again." Mel looked down and his books, his head shaking.

There was more Steve wanted to say, but why re-open old wounds?

After that occurrence he had hurried back to his office, still experiencing embarrassment for having to deliver that lecture to Mel. There was work waiting to be done, papers strewn on his desk waiting to be read, some waiting to be signed. But he was immobilized, unable to shake the feeling, the resentment of the injustice woven throughout Lundery's dictatorial rants. He had continued staring, blankly, out the office window for a long while that day. He remembered speaking to himself in a whisper, "Someday, John, I will spit on your grave."

At the sharp caws of three overhead crows, Steve's mind returned to the present, to the rows of crosses, stone plates, and bronze plaques that stretched beyond his vision. As he looked down at the weathered mat of brown and green turf that covered the final resting place of John Lundery, he knew the day had come, the opportunity for retribution was here, but he found his feelings had evolved. His anger had turned to pity.

He thought back to those glimpses from his office door of John strutting through the halls like a prince, setting his kingdom straight, leaving a trail of animosity. Here, standing beside his grave, he began to see him in a new light. Now he understood: John had never grown up.

He should have guessed at John's demons from his remarks made at odd moments, from the frequent strange one-on-one discussions in the parking lot when John would catch him alone and share random glimpses of his life. John never said it outright, but he always left the impression he was asking for reassurance that his actions, his decisions were fitting and in keeping with his position in the organization.

John mentioned one day, for an unknown reason, that he was an only child. Steve could visualize John Lundery, a ten-year old, marching through his home, surveying his possessions, counting them, putting them in their proper place—*his* selected place.

Then there was John's story of how he had bought the plans and the wood to build a small end table for his first home. When the table was finished, he discovered it lacked uniformity in the shapes of the legs, and the edges were jagged. He told Steve he didn't waste time attempting to make adjustments. Almost bragging, he said, "It wasn't right; I smashed it."

That was long ago. Those were the actions, the words, of a man plagued by a need to be perfect. To make that happen, everything surrounding John Lundery had to be perfect. He was impelled to continuously overcome some inadequacy that the world must never see.

Steve discovered he no longer had the desire to spit, to scorn the remains beneath him; an offer of compassion would be appropriate. He had the power to forgive.

He heard a soft knell, probably from a service at the small chapel he passed driving in. He looked at his watch, thinking about the time, Nervous, he moved his foot, knocking away small pebbles and clumps of dirt. As he looked down, a message came, a thought he did not speak. It seemed appropriate. *John, you are there, forever still, with no stage to act out your ambitions; I continue here, alive, freed of those ambitions. That's all that matters, John. Rest in Peace.* Then he voiced his thoughts, loudly, with only the crows to hear him: "You won't make it into my book, John. Sorry."

The drive home took a little more than an hour. The traffic had not been too hectic, but a fatigue he not experienced before overcame him. Evelyn was out somewhere; he took a nap.

Fortunately, at dinner, Evelyn did not question him about his trip to the cemetery. Perhaps because she found him to be unusually sullen. He was having regrets about missing the opportunity to view his father's grave.

His fit of ill-humor persisted through the evening. Working on his book was the last thought on his mind. Evelyn seemed somewhat surprised, but again said nothing when he walked quietly into the living room and sat next to her on the couch to watch a two-hour movie on television.

As the end credits appeared on the screen, she handed Steve the remote, left the room and headed down the hall to dress for bed.

Steve turned off the television and retired to the kitchen where he found an old bottle of chenin blanc on the floor of the pantry, a bottle that he thought he had emptied months ago. He filled a tall stem glass with the wine, set it very carefully on the table and pulled out a chair into which he lowered himself equally carefully.

He raised the glass to his lips, tasting the liquid more than drinking it. As he sat, with his fingers on the base of the glass stem, he brought up the memory of the cemetery to revisit the primary remembrances of his trip: his brother's grave, the over-dressed elderly man, and the headstone announcing the presence of John Lundery.

The wine added to his fatigue as he expected. His pajamas, taken from the bedroom closet, were a jumble, but he was able to put his arms and legs through the right openings. In the faint glow of the nightlight he could see Evelyn, stretched out, motionless, the blanket up to her chin. With as little disturbance as possible, he lowered himself under the covers beside her. With his eyes closed, the light patterns sometimes seemed to form images. He was very, very tired. He did not recognize what the colors were forming. The bedroom seemed to be disappearing.

BACK ROADS

FACING the door to what he took to be a convenience store, a small structure, odd-looking and unknown to him, he strained to make out the name printed on the glass panes, a jumble of letters that did not make sense. Over his shoulder he could see a drive-through fenced with three fuel pumps. He found himself at a remote gas station. Why had he traveled here?

As he pulled the door wide and walked in, the slanted rays of the morning sun spilled along the aisles between food shelves stocked with potato chips and candy bars. Several women in dark clothing were bending toward the shelves, examining cans. At the rear of the store, against the wall, were refrigerated cases with tiers of shelves on which stood colored cans and bottles, like soldiers in formation, in wide rows, shoulder to shoulder, Illuminated by a cold, white light.

He walked to one case, opened the glass door, and took a chilled bottle of water from the shelf. He turned and placed the bottle on the counter where a clerk was talking on the telephone. He reached into a pocket for his wallet. It was not there. It must have fallen to the floor in his car. He let the bottle remain on the counter and walked outside to stand next to a gasoline dispenser where he could check the area.

His hand shaded his eyes from the clear, bright sun as he surveyed the vehicles lined up on the side of the small building. His car was not where he was sure he had parked it. How could that be? Maybe he had pulled into the back lot. Could it have been stolen in that short time? He walked over the cracked pavement to the rear of the building. There were several automobiles, but no white ones. His white car was always easy to spot.

He will have to call somebody for a ride. How could he explain his missing car? Where *was* he exactly? The two-lane road that fronted the store ran through featureless countryside devoid of any buildings, a gray streak that disappeared into a cloudless, intensely blue sky. Tall brown grass, intermixed with seed stalks, swaying to the beat of unheard music, covered the land on both sides of the road.

He reached into his right breast pocket for his cell phone. It was not there. Did he leave that on the car seat, too?

The clerk inside will surely let him use the store phone; he will give him a nice tip for his trouble. Wait. He had no wallet. He walked back to the door. With a steady tug on the discolored handle, the door opened slowly; he stepped inside. The clerk was not there. The women he had seen moments ago were gone. The cans and boxes on the shelves were intermixed and in disarray. What kind of a place *was* this?

He left the store again and walked to the edge of the highway. He could very well hail a passing car. A truck driver could be counted on to stop. One had helped him, that dreadful night in the past, when the fuel line on his old station wagon had broken and the gas tank ran dry. He had leaned against the car at the side of the road in the dark, trying to stay visible, his arm in the air, praying for deliverance. In five minutes, a rig he waved down rumbled up and halted to a stop a foot away. He got a ride home.

The road to his left was empty and without sound. A moment later, in the distance where the road crested, a tiny object appeared that grew larger and took the shape of a small truck the color of a coral bead. As it neared the gas pumps, it slowed and pulled off the road, bounced across the gravel shoulder toward him, nearly clipping the metal sign listing the gasoline prices, stopping beside it. The driver's door opened; a woman wearing a black cap emerged. The brim hid the upper part of her face, but he knew who she was—Bernice. As she walked toward him, she adjusted her cap, looking from side to side.

As she glanced at him, a tingle of excitement ran through him; he was terribly, terribly glad to see her. The question arose as to why she should be here, at this spot, at this time. Then, as he watched her familiar body movement, her confident stride, he relaxed, accepting that her arrival was perfectly understandable and predictable. He called out in a strong voice, "Are you here to give me a ride?"

She stopped short, smiled broadly at him, then walked carefully over the cracked cement to the gas pump where he stood. Now, faking innocence, she answered. "Why, do you need one?"

"I might." Her appearance was not what he remembered. "Bunny, what's that outfit you're wearing?"

She raised her arms and turned slightly like a fashion model to display her clothing: a light-weight, amber sweatshirt and gray trousers. "My shirt goes with the truck, don't you think?"

"A good match."

She let her arms fall; her palms slapped her thighs. "These are called travel pants."

"Why do you need those?"

"Cuz we're going to do some traveling. Get in the truck."

He was struck by the directness of her words. An offer like that required a little thinking. Where was she planning to go? Being out in the middle of nowhere didn't give him many choices. He turned toward the highway again. It was deserted. Why were there no cars? He could end up standing there forever.

He tipped his head. "Okay, let's go."

Back at the truck Bernice hopped into the driver's seat. Steve stopped to examine the door handle, fascinated by the blend of infinitely small specks of light that combined to form a brilliant copper-like finish. He opened the door and maneuvered into the soft seat.

Bernice fired up the engine; the truck bounced back onto the road.

Dare he ask? "Where are we headed?"

Her shoulders went up in a shrug. "I don't know."

"What do you mean, you don't know?"

"We're magic-roading."

"What's that?"

"I learned that from my daddy. When I was very, very little we would get in his car and head out into the countryside. When I would ask where we were going, he would say 'Wherever this route takes us, sprite. It's a magic road.'"

"That sounds like fun."

"It was." Her eyes shifted from the windshield to his face. "You know why I told you that, don't you?"

He hesitated answering. "I'm not sure."

"Those drives with my father were an important part of my life. I want you to make them part of the book."

"If you say they are that important, I will."

She seemed to question his sincerity. "Didn't you ever take long drives with your father?"

"As a matter of fact, you reminded me of the times my dad taught me a little about driving."

She brushed her nose with her finger. He had noticed her do that in the coffee shop—a nervous habit. She brushed it again as she said in a strained murmur, "Those were times I think about a lot. They get to me, you know." Her voice cracked. "I'd give anything to have just one more drive with my magnificent father." He watched her tighten her grip on the steering wheel.

She took a breath and asked, "On your trips, did your mother go along?"

"Sometimes."

Now she was smiling. "My dad would reach over and squeeze me like this." Bernice took her right hand off the steering wheel and clamped it on Steve's shoulder. He wondered if he were filling in for her father.

Her face grew somber. "Sometimes he would pat my knee." Again, she let go of the steering wheel and this time touched Steve's leg. As simple and harmless as it was, he was surprised by the familiarity. The weight of her palm communicated more than a friendly touch. Was it? Maybe she was making a pretense of innocence. Focusing on the bends in the road, she did not turn his way.

Ahead was an endless length of the gray paving, unbounded stretches of tall, beige grass and cloudless blue sky on either side. There were no buildings in sight. Bernice was driving with such calm confidence he was sure she had a destination in mind, that she knew exactly where she was headed.

Her face was fixed on the road ahead, but he knew she was looking at her father. She began smiling again for no reason. "My dad liked cigars," She said. "He didn't smoke in the house, because my mom objected—they were kind of strong, but he would smoke when we drove. He didn't buy cheap ones. I loved the smell of his cigars. The smoke mixed with the air blowing from his open window. It would send a tiny puff my way. Gee, it was like perfume."

As time and miles passed, the scenery, sun-drenched, open, weed-covered fields, never varied. It seemed to him they were headed in the wrong direction. He growled his growing concern. "I need to get home sometime today."

"What's the rush?"

"Nobody knows where I am."

The truck swallowed up the road, weaving left and right, mile after mile. Bernice seemed calm and comfortable, not troubled as he was by the absence of signs, crossroads, people, or vehicles.

Finally, to the right, in the distance, the landscape changed. The sky had become a deeper blue. Clouds had formed by the hundreds, a scattered lot of shrunken, uniform, pure white puffs, with little projections like legs and tails: a herd of sheep overhead.

A small grove came into view, a tight cluster of dark green, perfectly shaped trees. As they approached the picturesque setting, a narrow gravel entrance appeared. Bernice turned in and parked under a tree.

Steve tapped his thumb on his door window in the direction where he stared, frowning. "Is this where you wanted to go?"

"Never been *here* before."

She unhooked her seat belt and swung her head side to side, appraising the layout, smiling. "What a discovery. This place was put here for us, Steve. We can rest in the shade, talk, and there's nobody to see us or interrupt us."

The knowing came quick; she had corralled him again. "I take it your showing up was not a coincidence."

"I wanted to get out and about. A little side trip to give you a lift made it worthwhile. Aren't you glad you're not stuck at that gas station back there?"

How did she know how to find him? He did not respond. Her question brought up an image of the bottle of chilled water, sitting on the counter, miles away at the strange store, glistening with pearls of condensate, tempting him. He should have taken it with him when they left. It was what he needed now, a cold drink. Maybe down the road another store is waiting.

He asked, "Did your father ever get lost?"

"You mean when we were together in his car?"

"Yeah. Did you ever run into dead ends or find yourselves on a route that took forever to find a way out?"

"No. I always knew my dad would get us home. It was marvelous. And there were always shops along the way that sold candy or ice cream. He would stop and buy me a big cone. Somehow that ice cream tasted better than anything I can get now. Can you see me licking a big scoop of chocolate ripple?"

"Yes." He gave her a faux expression of intense awareness. "That was obviously a treat too joyous to forget."

"Very much so, Steve." She stopped smiling and looked at him, her brow pinched. "Please describe in your book what you envision about me in those places—an appreciative little girl, sitting next to her dad at a soda fountain, slurping frozen desserts."

"I think I can imagine what it was like. I never told you about my job as a soda jerk when I was in high school." He was poised to talk, but she wasn't listening.

"Oh, yes, high school," Bernice mumbled glumly, looking lost in an unpleasant thought. "A lot of interesting things happened in high school." Her tone clearly matched the intentional sarcasm.

Steve prodded her, "Tell me about them."

"There were some fun times, not a lot. I had only a few friends. There was something about the atmosphere of the school that ruined four years of my life. No, I take that back; it wasn't the school; it was Paula."

"Paula?

"Paula Brunfeld. She ran a huge clique, most of the better-looking girls. I wasn't part of it."

"Weren't you good-looking enough?"

"She avoided me because I saw through her. She had an air of phony superiority; her clan prized her because she passed along a lot of gossip, a lot of which she made up."

Steve sensed the anger building in her. "And you were not the type to play along."

"I caught her at it one day. She was furious. She didn't like me listening to her. So, she invented her own language, a kind of pig-latin that she began using to hand down her super secrets to her disciples when they met on the campus."

Bernice rolled down her window; the air drifting in was warm. Her head swung side to side as she inspected the small forest. "There are no birds," she reported, in a distressed voice. "I watch birds a lot."

She asked, "Would you like to get out and walk a little?"

He wanted to get moving, get to someplace familiar. He felt naked without his wallet and phone. Something had to be said, but not about his concern of being stranded. "I'd rather sit here and tell you about some memories I had forgotten."

"What are those?"

"When I was in high school, I had no girlfriends. Sure, there were several young ladies I had my eyes on. And I spoke to them often about the class material or school events, but that's as far as it went. I gave up on myself as being attractive to any of the girls. Then one day Patricia Halpet cornered me in the hallway at school. She was not fragile or petite; she was as tall as me, large-boned, sturdy you might say. She told me she was a member of some girl's club; I don't remember the name. They were planning a dance; Paper Moon was the theme. The club members were instructed to be bold, to ask the boys for dates. So, Patricia had chosen me. Almost apologetically, she asked me if I would be her date. I was overcome. I immediately agreed."

"I guess that improved your image of yourself."

"And listen to this, Bunny. I told her I didn't have a driver's license and would have to arrange for a taxicab to get her to the dance. She told me not to worry; her brother would come and pick me up."

Trying to control her laughter, Bernice said, "That's a good way to get a date. I never tried that. How did it work out?"

"I felt strange as I paced the floor at my house, waiting for my date to come for me. I figured it should have been the other way around. Patricia and her brother arrived on time; we took off. I must say, we all had a good time. There were some other nice-looking girls I would have liked to have tried the foxtrot with, but I made sure every dance for me was with Patricia."

"I'm sure you made her happy."

Steve remained silent, expecting Bernice to comment further. She rested her head on her fist and smiled, apparently content to just watch him and let him do all the talking.

Thinking she might want to suggest again that they leave the truck and stroll among the trees, he began gesturing and talking. "I recently met a fellow named Ron, a guy I once worked with. We had the same boss, a very unpleasant man."

"So, you exchanged some remembrances?"

"Unfortunately."

"And now you want to tell them to me so you can add them to the book."

He knew where she was headed. This was a hint that he was expected to include a scene, taking place in this truck, a scene with Phyllis rapturously attentive to Ray's narration of his embittering confrontations with his manager.

"I'm not sure those events should be in the book."

"Why not?"

"For two reasons. The first—and it may not be likely—is that some of his subordinate managers will recognize the circumstances, put the blame on me, and come after me for making a strictly company matter transparent."

"You mean accuse you of libel?"

"Well, I wouldn't use his real name, but they'd know who I was writing about."

"I think you worry too much. What's the second reason?"

He recalled his conversation with Ken Bretsom, the helpful author. He remembered spilling out how he was torn by a need to tell about the tyrants in his life and by an equally compelling desire to put them all to rest. "I've already put in a lot of negative material. But I'm having second thoughts. I want the book to paint a picture of a life that was fulfilling, not be an exercise in revenge."

"Don't think of it that way. Everybody goes through those periods when life isn't fair. In your book, use those unpleasant circumstances to your advantage; show how your character, Ray, overcomes them."

"Maybe you're right." He raised his left arm instinctively to check his wrist watch. It was gone. He interrupted Bernice's fascination with the clouds. "What time is it?"

"I don't know."

"Don't you have a clock on the dash?" He leaned over to peer through the steering wheel. The dashboard was solid black plastic. No speedometer, no gas gauge, no clock. Confused, he asked, "How do you drive this buggy? You could get a ticket for speeding.

She ignored his remark. "I've had a few of my own bitter lessons in the workplace."

"You never told me what you did."

"I worked for a company that made airplane parts. I wrote procedures for several departments. I was very young." As she spoke, she looked at something far away.

"Were you any good?"

"Oh, yes. The time I spent in college paid off. I was very good. In fact, it was that job that got me to thinking about becoming an author—writing my own books."

"Was that a happy time for you?"

"Very. But there were a few bad times."

"Are you working up to tell me about those times?"

"Not much to tell. You know the old saying; you forget the pleasant things and remember all the bad stuff."

"What happened?"

"It was my first job after my divorce; I took some writing classes and was hired as a technical writer for an aircraft parts company—important defense stuff. I worked for a man named Bernie Grosink." A shadow of a large bird crossed the windshield. Bernice broke off her tale and poked her head out of her window.

She continued. "One day Bernie told me that the company was on a productivity kick. Some executive would be named as Productivity Team Leader. Douglas Helmwil, a director, ended up as the stuckee. Helmwil sent out notices to all the managers—like Bernie—to get employees in their groups to submit ideas for increasing productivity. I volunteered. Another new technical writer in Bernie's group, Neal Archet, also signed up to contribute some material."

He laughed. "Didn't you guys ever hear the rule about never volunteering? That's what I learned in the Navy," He laughed again. "What fired you up on the subject?"

"Youthful enthusiasm, I guess. I spent several days, often on my own time, Steve, writing pages of managerial strategies for productivity using material that I had learned in business courses I took. Neal did the same thing."

"And you were awarded a medal."

"Quite the opposite."

With lips pressed tightly together, Bernice laid back, staring at the roof of the cab.

"Bunny, you have to tell me how it ended."

"A week later, Bernie called me into his office. I saw my productivity essay lying on his desk. He pointed at it. He wasn't smiling as usual."

Bernice shook her head in disbelief. "Bernie said he was furious. He told me Helmwil had returned Neal's and my write-up with a note. He pushed my essay over to me with obvious disgust, and asked me to read what Helmwil had written."

"What did it say?"

"I remember looking at Helmwil's handwriting. God, I was angry. My blood pressure must have gone up forty points."

"What did it *say?*

She shook her clenched fist. "It was addressed to Bernie. It said *I think you have a problem in your department.*"

"What did you make of that?"

He watched her slowly open and close her fist, the edges of her mouth drawn back in anger. "We were being informed that directors don't want to be told how to manage. Productivity is the responsibility of the worker bees."

"How did you take it?"

"It bothered me for several days; I was overcome with a terrible feeling of suppression." Bernice slid down a little in the seat, her hands patting the steering wheel.

Steve groped for a response, something. "The dean of the business school at my college gave a long speech on management. What stuck was his warning to managers: praise fades quickly, but small hurts are long remembered."

She pivoted her head as if to shake away a thought. "I wanted to give up putting words on paper."

"But you overcame that, as you suggested Ray should."

"I did." She sat up, animated. "I remembered something miss Stevenson at the high school told me, something positive, something I've carried all my life. She was the faculty advisor for the school newspaper. I had written a fun piece about students being handed out class assignments over the holidays—it was just satire—but one of the teachers complained that it was offensive." She looked down and shook her head again, painfully.

In the silence that followed, he placed his hands on the dashboard, looked out at the motionless trees, and took a deep breath. He knew she was re-living a moment that was long gone, but ever fresh in that place in her mind where those little, useless, and sometimes objectionable, trinkets are stored—like his garage. "I'm sure the very resourceful Bunny took action."

His comment woke her. She said, "I apologized to the teacher and pled my case to miss Stevenson. In a very understanding way, she told me that no matter how pure my intentions are, there will always be somebody who will object to what I write."

He sensed the power that her recollection had over her. "I can understand why that episode is significant to you. I will put it in the book."

Small lines appeared around her eyes; her voice was gentle. "I want you to promise."

"I promise."

"By the way, how's the book coming?"

Steve held up his hands and wiggled his fingers, as though typing. "I've been doing lots of writing, but sometimes I think I'm not putting enough life into the words."

Bernice began to grimace. He continued. "I'm not impressed with what I'm reading—page after page of conversation. It's getting to be all talking."

She put her arm over his shoulder. He tensed, expecting to be drawn closer. The arm only rested there, adding emphasis to her words. "Don't worry about that. Keep it simple. Write what happened. These things we talk about aren't made up, Steve; it's stuff from our hearts. What we did, what we said long ago is important to us. The people who read your book will sense that importance." She removed her arm and looked at him soulfully.

What he heard sounded good, but he was not convinced. He turned away and stared blankly through the dusty windshield at the hood of the truck, a gleaming bronze shield in the sun. "I'm still not sure that's all it takes, Bunny. I haven't read good fiction all that much—I admit. Even the little sampling I have done recently, however, has made me very aware that first-class authors include a lot more description of the location where everything is happening and what else is going on around the people in the story. That stuff is lacking in what I have written. I'm not good at that, Bunny; I'm not seeing things."

At his words her eyes opened wide, almost to a glare; her head lowered slightly; her voice solemn as that of a judge handing down a life sentence. "Your job, Steve, is not to write the Great American Novel. Your job is to finish the manuscript you started."

She watched his reaction. His lack of agreement told her he was still casting about for words to support his concern.

She continued her harangue. "I know what you're going through, Steve, but your book has everything it needs. You've got to stop nursing it. Cut it loose and share it with the world." She looked away with a jerk, her jaw tight.

Her lecture was finished, but he knew she had other expectations for him to fulfill. He shifted his weight, turned close to her, and rested his arm on the steering wheel. "Bunny, a lot has happened since you picked me up back there. Are you asking me to remember *all* of this? The rides with your father? The ice cream sundaes?"

"Yes, *all* of it." Her voice was surprisingly loud.

"And you want it all in my book?"

"It has to be. That's the way your reader learns we get to know more about each other, to care more."

"To care more?"

"That too."

She began humming the melody to "If I Didn't Care."

Steve said, "I know that song."

"I'm sure you do. I'm sure your father sang it for you."

"How would you know that?"

"You told me your father liked to sing. He sang to you."

"Yes, he did. That song goes way back. I'm surprised you ever heard it."

"It's from the late thirties. I heard it on a seventy-eight-rpm shellac disc my father kept. I think the music back then was more melodic, less complicated. I have a saying, Steve. *Old songs are the best.* Put *that* in your notebook."

He was about to question where this business of *caring* started and where she was going with it when she reached in front of him abruptly and dug into her pouch wedged between the front seats. She took out a folded slip and handed it to him, quietly explaining, "It's a poem I wrote for us. Read it."

He opened the small paper and looked at the neat, hand-lettered words.

Hey, Love

Hey, Love, I guess you'd say in this life,
We met too late.
But let's thank Fate for having met at all.
We started out with friendly conversation,
It wasn't in the plan for us to fall.

Only now and then,
Could we share the spark we found,
But, hey, Love, didn't we shake the ground.

She put her hand down and nipped the paper with her finger and thumb, tugging at it as she looked up at his eyes. "It would make a nice song, don't you think?"

His reaction was to say something cute about her branching off into poetry, but he really wanted to cut short whatever was going on here. He released his grip on the paper; it fell to the floor.

He confessed, "Bunny, as I put together my chapters, I'm trying to put a handle on the range of the places we meet and the bundle of memories you want me to pack in my book. Up to now, it's only been you and me."

"Yes, Steve. And that will work. You got me, babe—like the song says."

She seemed now to be suggesting he had made a commitment. He had considered her role in the telling of his life to be simply a foil, someone to throw memories at, a clever device. She seemed now to be harboring expectations far beyond his ability or desire to fulfill.

He had to level. "I know you don't want to hear this, Bunny, but there *are* other friends, relatives—people I worked with—that could share stories with me."

The lines that suddenly appeared above her eyes, the lost look, an aura of urgency, altered her features dramatically. "You don't understand, do you?"

She laid her hand on his shoulder and pulled him toward her with a smooth, steady motion. She held her head inches from his, her warm breath enveloping him; he did not resist. Eyes open, her face exhibiting a mood of both persuasion and submission, she closed the small distance and pressed her mouth against his, holding the kiss, it seemed, forever, communicating a thousand words.

He relaxed and let the experience engulf him. Her performance was too well-orchestrated to be spontaneous. The act was—yes—premeditated! The intriguing curvature and coloration of her cheeks commanded his view; he could feel every particle of the warm, intimate texture of her lips. Then she released him.

He fell back to the cushion, but it was no longer a truck seat, it was a soft pillow. Then he sensed the contours of the blanket and sheet that enclosed him.

AMPLE NARRATIVES

AS his eyes opened from the deep sleep, the familiar stippled pattern of the ceiling above him began to take shape. As he turned the blanket down from his chest, the folds caught his fingers. It was morning; he was home, in his bed. Bernice, the truck, the grove—all gone. The unsettling realization formed that what had just happened, the ride in the truck, the long conversations with Bernice—all of that—no matter how tangible, was another dream.

He could see her face close to his, every detail in the skin of her cheeks, the strands of her hair. The taste of her lips persisted; he could feel their pressure, the warmth. He struggled with the glowing reality of what had occurred; he had never felt physical contact with a human in any dream in his life. His hand rose and touched his mouth.

There was a small tremor in Evelyn lying beside him, but she was asleep. Could he have said anything while dreaming? Probably not. Ev would have given him a shove as she always did when he made a sound in the night.

He swung out of bed, standing somewhat unsteady. His legs were a little wobbly; something new to worry about. He eased himself back onto the edge of the bed. Maybe these were the signs of aging he expected twenty years from now coming to pay him an early visit.

The clock on the nightstand said seven. His thoughts kept pulling back to the dream. He didn't know what to make of Bernice's behavior. This was a problematic turn of events, an intimacy that left him slightly stunned. His mind was locked onto the image of her face, the burning touch of her kiss.

The only activity that he was capable of at that moment was making coffee. He will need a lot today. The dream had introduced some facets to Bernice he hadn't seen before. There was writing that had to be done, but he wasn't sure what to say or whether he was capable of saying it.

He rose again and stepped carefully down the hall to the kitchen, touching the wall occasionally for balance. He reached the counter where the coffee maker sat, bending down to check the level in the water gauge. It was full. Evelyn had done all the preparations the night before—bless her. He inserted the power cord in the socket and pushed the silver button. A tiny glass bead on the silver face of the machine glowed red. He reached up into the cupboard and took out two cups that he placed on the table. He left the kitchen, heading back to check on his wife.

When he entered the bedroom, Evelyn was awake, sitting up, leaning back on two pillows propped up against the headboard. She looked up from a book she was reading, let it fall to the blanket, and, with a touch of guilt, said. "I suppose you want to get some sleep."

He realized he must have looked groggy, but more sleep was the last thing he needed. "No, if you're enjoying yourself, continue."

"I will. This book is getting my attention."

"Which one is that?"

"The one you brought home from the book signing."

He faltered, straightened the bedsheet, plumped up his pillow, and strained to get a glimpse of the book's cover. What had he told her? "Is that the one by Ken Bretsom?"

"Yes."

"What do you think of it?" he asked.

"It's encouraging."

"What do you mean, encouraging?"

She displayed the open book to him. "I'm thinking *you* should be encouraged by it. Have you read any of it, yourself?"

"I'm embarrassed to admit I haven't."

"I'm sure you can do as well as he. It's written in a very simple, straightforward style. There are no elaborate sentences; he doesn't brag about any special accomplishments; it's just about an ordinary life. And you *did* say his books were best-sellers."

His head dipped in agreement. "Well, he had many fans at the book signing, and they *were* buying a lot of copies."

"Well, that tells you something."

"I guess you're right. I might be doing better than I realize. I'm glad you said that, Ev. I get hung up a lot. I keep thinking there's some great insight or revelation that should emerge from every little event in my life. You've got me in the mood for writing. I'll stop wasting time and finish a few pages today."

"I want to see you do that."

"Let's get dressed and go have breakfast," he said. He reached over and picked up the book she had placed aside, looking over what she had been reading. The words were simple; yes, he could do as well. That was all the encouragement he needed to proceed. He wanted to sit down and start writing, but his stomach reminded him that Evelyn will be preparing something delicious, and besides, whatever she cooked up will give him energy. He raised himself from the edge of the bed and stepped toward the closet. He hoped Evelyn had washed his favorite shirt.

After breakfast he picked up the morning newspaper from where it was lying on the counter and began reading the headlines again. Evelyn fumed, "Put that aside; get working." She chased him into the den with his coffee cup in one hand and the morning newspaper in the other. He threw the paper on the desk where it spilled apart.

As he sat at the computer, he looked at the pile of small pieces of paper next to the keyboard—notes to himself on story ideas—picking them up one at a time, checking the slip for inspiration, throwing it in the waste basket. Old stuff. The events of this morning's dream were on tap, nudging him. They had to be dealt with.

Bernice's encounter with diphtheria was clear enough and will be short in telling. He began to type. *Wait.* He stopped and raised his hands above the keyboard as if someone had tapped him on the shoulder. There was something dreadfully wrong with the timeline of Bernice's life. Even if she were forty, diphtheria would not have been a threat when she was a toddler. That epidemic raged thirty years before her possible birthdate. She said there were no medicines for the disease. That true in the nineteen thirties. There were other things she brought up from the past in their conversations. How could she be so familiar with seventy-eight-rpm phonograph records? She would have to be much older than she appears.

He opened his manuscript on the monitor and started typing. He looked at his words: "Patricia cornered him in the school hallway and spoke to him." He paused, drew his hands back, and let them fall in his lap. Who was he telling this to? Bernice, of course, but he hadn't written that in yet. Bernice had to brought into the scene again—somehow. She had to be there to listen. But, unfortunately, she also did a lot of the telling—and questioning. That was necessary. It was those questions that had pushed him into recalling the unpleasant regime of John Lundery.

On the other hand, she was crowding out some new, very private stuff he wanted to insert. But she insisted that *her* comments, her own, very complete, very personal disclosures *had* to be there as well. And there they were, right on the page before his eyes. If he deleted them, their conversations about their childhood, their schooling, their jobs, wouldn't make sense.

An awakening spilled into his mind: Bernice was exerting more control over the contents of the pages on the screen than he had planned. Another obstacle he will have to think about.

He slumped back in the chair, doing nothing more productive than observing his breath, thinking, maybe, there were some other priorities to be tended to. There was no trace of the enthusiasm that usually arrived with the morning coffee. He needed something to get his imagination active.

His eyes fell on the newspaper next to his coffee cup; surely one small peek at the sports section was permissible. He found the section with the photos of the players all suited up, and spread the pages open over the keyboard. He smoothed the page with his hand, looking for his favorite teams. At the bottom of the box listing the football scores was an ad. The word DREAMS immediately blocked out everything else he was thinking about. He examined it carefully. The ad read "Dreams analyzed by experienced psychic, Velda Lasseur. Madame Lasseur has testimonials from hundreds of clients that her readings align with their lives." A telephone number was given. The ad guaranteed a fifteen-minute telephone conversation would answer any and all questions about the events of a caller's dream. The charge was twenty-five dollars, payable by credit card.

He rested his hand on the desk phone, tapping one finger. A call to this "Velda" might turn something up—or at least be fun. She could be a fake, but then her questions and her answers will tell whether she was really on to something. She might surprise him. She just might sense something about his memories he didn't know. He granted there are people with those abilities. She might actually figure out who Bernice was.

There was a downside though. The prospect of talking to a stranger, opening up about personal matters, about dreams he hadn't even told Evelyn about—that required a little forethought. Madame Lasseur might press him to tell about other women he had known well. Would she get him to admit he found himself physically attracted to Bernice? Would he have to explain why she kissed him?

He took his hand from the phone, folded the newspaper and stuck it in the wastebasket. The overriding flaw in this foolish venture will be having to explain the phone call when Evelyn checked the monthly credit card statement and asked, "Who is this 'Velda' you paid twenty-five dollars to?"

He had to smile that he had even considered talking to a self-proclaimed psychic. There were too many down-to-earth tasks waiting for him. The spark of enthusiasm ignited again. He began typing. He felt good about it; the doubts about ever completing his project fell away. His father had reminded him often to be thankful for whatever fate made available—and to *use* it.

He discovered that when he made for himself a quiet place at the desk, when he stilled his mind, there was an unlimited stock of word pictures out there, somewhere, for him to draw upon. As though it was his father's voice counseling him, a thought arose—an affirmation—one that he will call up again at the hint of any uncertainty that he could finish: *I am grateful for this opportunity; I will not waste it.* He glanced at his notes. In the silence of the den, the images in his mind became very sharp. He leaned forward, lightly fondling the keyboard. As the words flowed to his fingertips, line after line of prose appeared on the page. The commitment to feed this fire of creativity to its end took hold.

Each day of the weeks that followed, with an occasional urging from Evelyn, Steve pounded away, becoming one with his word processor, creating, in words, the world he had lived; the manuscript grew and took shape. During the early weeks, very little thought was given to Bernice, and eventually none at all.

There were no more dreams of Bernice. He now looked back at them as an anomaly. Sure, he was working from notes about their discussions, but mention of her grew automatic; the woman with whom he shared his stories became just another character on the page. The dreams that had stolen his attention were a remnant of the past.

Evelyn walked by the den door, paused and cleared her throat to get his attention. "Are you going to do some late-night writing?"

"Nope, I'm done."

"All done. Really?"

"Yes, I'm actually mulling over the title." He laughed. "Would you believe that is the hardest part of the whole damn book."

"Don't you even have one that might work?"

"Oh, I have a tentative one. I'll tell you later."

"I might read a little in bed. Will that bother you?"

"No. I don't fall asleep easily anyway."

Evelyn lifted and examined a pair of pajamas draped over her arm. "I'm leavin'. Turn down the thermostat before you get to bed." She walked away.

Steve rolled his chair next to the desk and picked up two open envelopes lying there. From each he shook out the papers inside and snapped them up. He grabbed the desk edge, pulled himself from the chair, and left for the closet.

Steve entered the bedroom, dressed for sleep in his red plaid pajamas. He carried the two sheets of paper which he placed on the blanket as he dropped to the edge of the bed, jarring it vigorously. Evelyn was stretched out in her place, propped against her bed rest, reading a book by the warm light from her seashell lamp on the nightstand. The jerky movement got her attention.

She lowered her book to the bed and gave a casual, almost sleepy look at the papers. "Is that something you want to show me," she asked.

"Yes," he said. "It's about my book."

"Good news or bad news?"

Smiling at her amazingly appropriate question, he replied, "It's a little of both."

"Well give me the good news first."

"Do you remember me telling you I sent a couple chapters of my book to that Linda Kosolow? She's the literary agent that Ken Bretsom, the writer, referred me to."

She became very attentive. "Yes, yes, go on."

He waved the paper victoriously. "She wrote me that she found a publisher for my book."

"Hurray!"

"I won't read you the details. Whoever at the publisher checked my material first was ready to reject it. The comments were that the story had no unusual or adventuresome elements, and I was a complete unknown. But one of the other book editors happened to look through it and thought it had promise. He told Mrs. Kosolow that although they look for stories with more energy and more intricate plots, mine had *charming innocence*."

"So, you're going to mail her your complete manuscript"

"I'm ready to do that, but I have to tell you about this other letter."

"The bad news?"

"Well, not really. It's from Ken Bretsom. I had sent him the same two chapters that I sent Kosolow. I told him he wasn't obligated to read them and comment. While he was still sitting on them, I heard from Kosolow and I wrote Ken that I got her approval; I said I didn't need his help. But—bless him—he sent his comments anyway." Steve waved the second piece of paper.

"So, what's the bad news?"

"Ken wrote back that he was truly glad my story approach was accepted, but he thinks it will garner more sales if I spruce it up a little."

"What does he suggest?"

Steve's face grew a little contorted. He waved his hands as he groped for an exact answer. "He thinks it needs a little more . . . precision . . . in the descriptions of the settings where the conversations in the novel take place."

"I know what he means, Steve. I could show you some examples in this very story I'm reading now." She held up the book. "Did he have any other tips?"

"Yeah. He believes I missed opportunities to inject more emotions into many of the recollections of the really significant events—goof-ups when I was young, frustrations on my job. He said there must have been a lot more anger or joy at those moments. To use his words, they didn't happen in a vacuum."

"Can you do all those things?"

"I admit he has a point, but it will take going back over every page and thinking through each paragraph."

She grabbed his arm to drive her point home. "Well, you've worked on your book for almost four months. Another week or two shouldn't matter."

"That's a decision I'm wrestling with."

In a very upbeat tone she said, "I think whatever you do will work out. Tackle that worry in the morning."

She placed her book on the nightstand and lifted a small clock, squinting at the hands. "It's later than I thought. Let's hit the hay."

She turned a switch on the lamp base, her corner of the room went dark. She placed the bed rest on the floor, laid back, and pulled the covers up to her chin. "Good night, get some rest."

He switched off the lamp on his side and worked his way under the blanket. "I will. Good night to you, too."

His eyelids relaxed and closed, shutting off his view of the dimly lit seashell serigraph on the wall, Evelyn's cherished find at the art auction. His mind, drawn to the stack of deliberations awaiting him tomorrow, began to stir.

Kosolow, his agent—and he liked using that term—asked him to think about ways he could promote his novel once it hit the bookstores. He owed her an answer. Now he started hearing that small voice that nagged him to follow Ken Bretsom's advice on punching up some of the scenes.

But perusing this mental shopping list could keep him awake all night. Besides, failing to doze off quickly was getting to be a recurrent problem. It seemed that old age had hidden the switch that would put him into sound sleep in a minute—a feat that came easy in the Navy. Maybe because he had no worries then and usually worked his tail off aboard ship.

That was it. He just needed to get back in the condition of a young bluejacket. Starting tomorrow, during the day, he will imagine he hears the bugle call to General Quarters, the starter gun for the flight to his battle station—wherever that is.

The word "sleep" brought up his memory of the impressive Dr. Dohlstram's willingness to share his research into conquering insomnia. "You might think of it as meditation," Richard had said. "Try this: focus on your breathing. Feel the air entering your nostrils, or notice the rising and falling of your chest. Or look at the play of muted colors behind your closed eyes. To put it simply: stop thinking."

Okay doc, Steve conceded. He chose to monitor the thumping of his heart. The beats were strong and regular. That was comforting; at least his heart will last him the night. He kept his attention there for several minutes. Was this working?

An image came, he was in a large field—a war-torn No Man's Land perhaps—perforated with waist-high concrete projections that resembled the Dragon's teeth of World War II. No, it was not a battlefield. The objects sprouting from the ground were curved and decorative. Small furry creatures scampered playfully and unafraid. He looked more closely at the peaceful place he found himself in.

PAYING RESPECT

TWO squirrels, their matching coats a strange mixture of dark and light fur, paused in the coarse gravel in front of the wooden bench on which he sat, as if discussing where an acorn might be waiting, then scampered straight up the broken, rough, gray bark of a black alder next to him. Although the interplay of the tiny animals he watched was not unusual, something seemed strange, out of place.

Once the squirrels had gone, Steve twisted and began examining the bench on which he rested. It looked new. The slats were clean and smooth, the color of cedar. Probably beechwood. As he rubbed his hand across the surfaces, his eye caught the lettering on the backrest: *In Loving Memory of Emily Presrig.*

The realization came abruptly; this was a cemetery. What brought him here? In the distance, here and there, marking ownership of patches of soil, were crosses, some white, some the color of the earth on which they stood. There were large irregular slabs of polished stone bearing names, sharing the field with the scattered, tarnished metal vases of limp flowers. The air was unusually warm for December. He looked down at his arms. He was wearing a light jacket. He reached with both hands in the pockets on both sides. His wallet was missing. Unease set in.

There was no path visible; he was surrounded by matted grass flecked with the last of the curled brown leaves given up by the trees in the December chill. Where was the way out of here? Where was his car?

To his far right a woman in a long-sleeved black dress of heavy material was bending over a grave. She might know the way to the parking area. He rose from the bench and walked carefully over the uneven soil to where she stood. As he reached her, she straightened up stiffly, acknowledged his presence with a casual look, as if she'd known he was there all the time. She said, somewhat sternly, "Good afternoon, Steven; it's about time you arrived."

Her words immobilized him; he could only stare. It was Bernice, but it wasn't Bernice. She had never dressed this formally. She was not wearing her usual contagious smile. Her demeanor was somber as she waited for his reply. In all of their previous meetings, there was always a carefree air about her. But now, at this moment, she seemed occupied with something, some mission.

"Why are you here?" he asked.

"To tie up some loose ends, as the saying goes." She didn't look up from the graves as she spoke. Her answer was solemn and cryptic.

He couldn't dismiss the hunch that she was here to tell him something. "Did you have more stories for me?"

"I have no more stories. Why, do you need some?"

"No, it occurred to me that there might be one last incident that you never had a chance to relate. I'm relieved though that you don't. I think my book is almost finished."

She turned quickly toward him; her face taut. "You *think*?"

"Everything is there I wanted to say, Bunny, everything we talked about. I might have done a better job of saying it. I guess I'm reaching for some inspiration, a fresh way to see things better."

He watched her eyebrows rise as she spoke. "That *will* take a while, won't it?"

She had never seen a word he had written, so how could she understand his predicament? If he could just hand her a single page of his manuscript to be read, the dull and labored parts that nagged him would become clear. "Yes, there are words and emotions I didn't mention that went along with those sad and happy times, Bunny, little bits of life that shaped me, things my readers ought to know."

She watched him speak, but he knew she wasn't listening; her ears seemed closed to any message pleading for support for the very purpose of their communions. This discussion was going nowhere. He looked away at the endless stretch of land that circled them, unfamiliar and discomforting, dotted with strangely shaped clumps of rock used for headstones. He should be home, not standing here in this remote nowhere; He should be sitting in a chair in his living room, reviewing his manuscript.

He felt obligated to further defend his point. "I'm really an amateur at this writing, you know. As I re-read the stuff I put down, I keep asking myself if I made those bygone days really come alive. I think one more pass will add a lot, Bunny." That sounded good. He thought that might convince her; he smiled.

She did not look pleased. "Steve, you talk as if you had all the time in the world. I can assure you that those hours will *not* be there; time is not an endless piece of thread you pull from the spool as you need it."

Her arms went out, her eyes down. She seemed to be lecturing the unhearing signposts of humanity that surrounded them. "There are stories I, Bernice Batelle, could have finished, pieces that would have told the world more about me. They were *good*, Steve, but I allowed myself to believe I could make them *perfect*. Oh, I could have, my friend. But instead, those weeks that I thought lie ahead, long weeks just waiting for my immortal prose . . . they arrived . . . and they stole the very means for me to deliver those perfect versions to the page."

With that, she raised her arms slowly, turned her palms toward her chest, fingers wide-spread, and stared at them, angrily, as though she didn't recognize them.

Steve threw his arms out and to the sides in an imploring display, countering. "I have to ask myself: have I been completely honest—did I make the effort to really describe how I felt about things? I don't expect my readers to be entertained by a résumé of how I grew old—thinking that I simply typed material as it occurred to me."

Her look became pure anguish. A swell of intense emotion had gathered in her expression as she spoke. "I'm sure your book is fine the way it is; put it to bed."

This was getting awkward. It was important that she understand what concerned him. He tried again. "Well, you have a stake in it too, Bunny. I only wanted the best."

There was no response from her to his words. He hoped she might back off but she continued to stare grimly. The silence was overwhelming; he raised his hand in surrender. "Okay, consider it done."

When he finished speaking, she relaxed. The edges of her mouth turned up the slightest bit. "That's good," she said. Then the tone of her voice softened, became almost cheerful. "I hope you did justice to your father in the book. I was thinking what a wonderful man he was."

"My father?" he said in a clearly questioning voice.

She ignored his reaction, became detached, motionless, as though she didn't hear him, but he knew she did. She leaned forward, inspecting the graves around her.

He asked again, with firmness, "Why do you mention my father? How would you know he was wonderful?"

She answered, casually, without looking back. "Because you told me so—many times."

With that she straightened up, stood tall, her eyes fixed on the distance, her head turning slowly as though tracing a remote, invisible arc that surrounded them.

Her answer left him questioning the reliability of his memory again. *My wonderful father? What had he ever told her?* His mind raced through an inventory of the episodes with his father he had related to her in the past. Sure, there were a couple of stories, but he had said nothing about his father's accomplishments at the air base, his awards in school. Or did he?

She began walking head down, as though fascinated by the shapes and colors of the fallen leaves. He interrupted her search. "What are you looking for?"

"His grave."

"Who's grave?"

"Arthur's."

"Why are we searching for my father's grave?"

"To pay our respects, love."

"It's not here, not where we are."

"I'm sure it is. Help me look."

He succumbed to a feeling of frustration and helplessness; his arms collapsed at his sides. He watched her step sideways, grave by grave, pausing and perusing the names, slowly, as though each held a meaning for her. She seemed unaware of him as she moved into the distance, searching. She stopped. Abruptly, her arm came up, indicating a patch of soil. "Here it is," he heard her say. Her voice was weak with a tone of almost sadness.

He took slow, careful steps to where she was pointing. Flat in the earth, obscured by small tufts of grass, was a worn, gray, oval piece of concrete. There were letters pressed into the rough surface: *Arthur Ribman.*

He looked closer. There was some mistake. *This is not his grave.* His father's resting place is marked by a large, beautiful, speckled gray marble tombstone that Alice helped pay for.

He looked over at Bernice, standing beside him. She had bent down, close to the small rock-like marker, as if to be assured of the name imprinted there. A slight tremor appeared in her head. Her hand drifted across the grave, as if in farewell, then came up to her eye to wipe something away. A tear perhaps. She said, weakly and haltingly, "Some will look at this grave, but none will know what this man did. He was a strong leader, but he was kind."

He chose not to express his distrust of this counterfeit-looking grave. "I appreciate your respect for my father, but how could you know how he spent his life?"

There was impatience in her voice as she kept her eyes on the grave, her head still shaking. "It all came out in what *you* have said about him, Steve."

Then she swung back in his direction, stared at him, and extended her hand. "I'm sure you turned out to be very much the man your father was. From the stories you told me, I came to know him." The frown lifted from her face. "When you speak, I hear him. When I look at you, I see him."

She turned again and walked toward a small stand of trees. When she reached the first one, she stopped and placed her hand high on the rugged trunk, looking up at the bounty of perfectly formed leaves, shivering but clinging securely to the coarsely arranged branches. "It's beautiful here," she said. She dropped her head down to gaze at Steve over her shoulder, sharing a very carefully formed sardonic smile. "One could almost look forward to residing forever in this place." Then she looked down to the base of the tree. She began reciting.

"Dust into dust, and under dust, to lie.
Sans wine, sans song, sans singer, and sans end."

Her eyes came up to watch his reaction. "Do you grasp its meaning?" she asked.

"I know that poem," he said. "I was lectured on it when I was too young know that it was talking to me."

For Steve, the words were like the overture to an opera. The sky, trees, matted grass, and somber shapes of the head stones disappeared. Another vision took over. Under the proscenium, on the brightly lit stage, there he was, sitting at his desk in high school. At the front of the class stood an alert, motivated young man, well-dressed in a white shirt and dark blue necktie, reading aloud in dramatic tones from a book he held open in his hands. He spoke some words loudly for emphasis, his eyes going up to Steve to see if they had registered with his audience.

"I know that poem," Steve repeated. "You've brought back some more memories, Bunny."

"Of course," she said. "But don't spend any more time on the book trying to find a place for them. They don't *have* to go in."

She fell back against the tree and reached behind to grasp it, steadying herself, letting her head rest on the bark as she viewed the sky.

"I think you know the reason we have found each other." she said. "It was a merciful fate that led me to you. Each of us has a song to sing, Steven, and each of us looked at the calendar, then the timepiece on the wall, and realized there are a short and finite numbers of days and clock ticks left for you and me to tell what we found when we woke to this world. I have helped you with the shape of your book and you have given me the place to store my confessions."

"I understand," he said.

She stepped away from the tree, gliding toward him effortlessly. She came up to him, close, putting her hands on his forearms, never taking her eyes from his. "My mission is finished, Steve. I won't be visiting you anymore."

A heavy cloud shrouded the sun. An unusually deep shadow moved across the area where he stood watching Bernice's face darken and darken. Then the light around him began to flicker. Something was changing.

STORY ELEVEN

CONNECTIONS

SHADOWS on the drapes came into focus. He jumped from the bed and slid his feet into the slippers lying askew on the carpet.

Evelyn, startled, moaned, "What is it. Another bad cramp?"

"Go back to sleep," he mumbled. "I just remembered where I left some information I need for my book. Gonna look for it. If I wait, I'll forget again."

That wasn't quite true, but it would do to explain his sudden frantic mission. He picked up a dark, green robe from the foot of the bed and threw it on. Staggering slightly, he swept out of the bedroom.

He brusquely pushed open the door to the garage, reached in and clicked a pad on the wall. A motor hummed above and the garage door rolled up. Along with a nippy gust of morning air, sunlight streamed in, bathing the walls, shelves, and their contents with intense radiation. He tugged at the sleeves of his robe, giving a thought to how he might appear to neighbors walking by. The street was empty.

He slid past Evelyn's car and began randomly pulling on cartons, checking the crude labels. There it was; the box marked DAD'S.

As he yanked the lids apart, he spotted the laminated penmanship certificate, the photo album, and the address book he had found when he searched the box in September. He lifted them out and placed them on the floor.

Now visible was the large brown envelope he was looking for. He lifted the flap, reached in and withdrew the small periodical. In the clear morning light, the print was exceptionally sharp. At the top was the name: "AFB CHRONICLE." On the front page was an article with the heading, "Air Force Base Recognizes Outstanding Employees." His father must have kept the paper because of something printed in the article that related to his work there. He scanned the text rapidly, looking for his father's name. There it was. After his name was the explanation: "He is the recipient of the Major Achievement Award for completing all assigned aircraft inspection reports ahead of schedule."

Filling the front page above the article was the large black and white photograph he was unable to examine fully that night when he first discovered the paper. Displayed was a group of seven men and three women. In the middle of the group, staring proudly out of the photograph, was Steve's father, holding up some kind of medallion on a ribbon. His eyes dropped down to the caption: "Arthur Ribman is honored for his wartime service at this airbase. The other workers in his department, shown above, agree that Chief Base Inspector Ribman is a source of pride and inspiration for them."

He began refolding the paper, pausing to scan once more the faces of the others attending the award ceremony. Awakened from his drowsiness, he was drawn to the features of one of the women, younger than the other two, but at least thirty-five. His lips moved, as if speaking. *Hold on.* There was something about her eyes, the mouth. He couldn't accept his reaction, but his vision was affirming that the woman standing there, the woman with a touch of a smile, was Bernice!

His eyes went up to the date on the top of the front page: September 15, 1944. He looked again at her face, studying it intently. There were no names of the people in the picture. Maybe it *wasn't* her.

What's going on here? He fell back against the car, letting his arm hang at his side, the newspaper loosely clipped by his fingers. A hundred thoughts competed for space in his brain, a hundred explanations, but the vision of her face crowded them all out. He thought about studying it some more, but he did not need to. That jaw, those eyes. It was Bernice. *Was it possible his father knew her?*

He did not want to draw a conclusion; he *could* not. If he had really examined this photograph years ago, it might have explained why a woman that worked with his father, a woman with clearly recognizable features, could appear in his dreams. But on that night in the garage he had only glanced at this newsletter, at this photograph, with no attempt to identify the faces shown. Unless . . . unless, as the shrewd Dr. Richard Dohlstram deduced, it had made a bigger imprint in his mind than he was aware of, an imprint that faded; a recurrence of a faulty memory he didn't want to accept.

A workable idea arose that pleased him; there might be names in the address book. With a swift motion he picked up and opened the small brown book labeled "Contacts." He started flipping pages and reading names. It was obvious his father had not entered them in alphabetical order. Here was a Marty Belchef. There were two numbers next to the name.

One was probably a home phone, the other possibly an extension at the air base. Here was another: Loren Shasta. Again, two sets of numbers. He turned back to the first page and looked at each name very attentively. Then, page by page, he ran his finger down the entries, stopping at each. Only ten pages had content. There were only two women's names, and they were of friends of his mother. If his father had reason to reach some of the people on his staff, why weren't the women listed?

A telephone call to Alice might explain things, a carefully worded call, of course. He will simply say, innocently, that he was going through dad's possessions that she had sent, and discovered the air base publication. He will mention, casually, that he accidentally came across the article about dad's award from the base, and was surprised, pleased, to discover that their father had been honored.

Alice might know a lot about his father's job. She conversed with him more often than he did in those years. After Steve was handed his diploma at high school, he had joined the Navy. His father had proudly accompanied him to the recruiting station. After he had filled out all the paperwork, his father, standing beside him, had thrown one arm over his shoulders, given him a firm hug, and said quietly, "You'll do all right. You'll make it."

But that enlistment had deprived him of the opportunities to pal around with his father as he had planned. He knew his sister was always there at their father's side during the years he was away in the Navy schools and at sea. She did all the talking and listening he had intended to do.

Yes, he will make the call to Alice, but how could he bring up Bernice, the woman in the photo?

Perhaps if he worded his questions cleverly enough, Alice might drop a clue.

He raised the newspaper again and scanned the other articles. There were announcements of safety meetings, cafeteria renovation—irrelevant stuff. Something caught his eye. At the very top of a page on a corner that was partially torn off were some handwritten words with some missing letters. The writing was unquestionably the ornate strokes of his father, flowing and distinct. He hadn't noticed them until now. He held the paper close. The remaining words were "Precious Moments Re . . ."

Something clicked. Where had he seen those words? Wasn't that a portion of book title? Yes. Those were some of the words on that tiny slip the library reference desk woman, Miss Wilkins, had given him—a book title, the words on the slip that got lost under Ken Bretsom's table at the library. Why would his father make a note of a book title on the same page as the photo?

When he walked back into the kitchen, he found the table set with the breakfast dishes. There were two plates and two croissants. Evelyn was at the range frying something. She looked over at him. "You spent a lot of time in the garage. I assume you're going to the office late."

"I'm taking the day off."

"Have a seat. Scrambled eggs are coming up."

He poured himself a cup of coffee and sat down. He waited for the question Evelyn will ask. She shoved a swirl of the eggs onto his plate. "Well, did you find what you were looking for?"

"Yes and no. I found some information about my dad's job at the airbase, a newspaper, but it didn't have a lot of detail."

Evelyn seated herself at the table and began buttering her croissant. "That's too bad. Was it something for your book?"

He hesitated. He put the coffee cup to his lips and held it there a moment while he thought of how he would answer. "Yes."

"I thought your book was about *you*. Why would you need information about your father's career?"

The questions were getting sticky. Evelyn knew that he spent very little time with his father during his years at the airbase, and she was aware he had never met any of his father's friends. How would he defend the need to have that kind of information for a novel based on his own life, his career and his friends?

He became irritated by his having to fall into this frequent evasiveness. He wanted to change the subject, but that would not pass. He gave her the answer she needed. "I thought that there might be some record of the work my father did during the war. You know, something that will dredge up memories of things we did together."

Steve noticed his hand moving his fork back and forth nervously. A Monday morning breakfast was always a time of cheerful review of the week gone by and the week ahead. He found himself terribly uncomfortable and he wasn't sure why. He had done nothing wrong, but he could not bring himself to say a word to Evelyn about the dream woman or her relation to his father.

At the top of the door leading to the patio Evelyn had tacked a spray of artificial juniper loaded with plastic holly berries and small silver bells. The display was an acceptable excuse to change the subject. He pointed up at the green branch over the frame. "Your Christmas décor is very attractive. Is it new?" he asked.

Evelyn rested her elbows on the table, tucked one fist under her chin, and looked aside in thought. "No. I bought it at a swap meet. I think it was two years ago. You were with me."

He continued with the tactic. "I guess I haven't been thinking about Christmas. What are we getting Robert?

Her eyes rolled. "Did you forget that too? Pajamas. I told you last week when I picked them out."

Her reference to his failing memory was not expected, an irritating reminder. He changed the subject again. "Do you have any plans for today?"

"Yes, unfortunately."

"What does that tone of voice mean?"

"Karen Stratferd, or should I say, her highness Karen, seems to have rounded up the last surviving members of our college sorority. We're having a holiday celebration this afternoon. I made the sad mistake of volunteering to pick out a cake, a few other things to eat, and deliver them. I'll probably be gone all afternoon. In fact, I'll be leaving in a couple of minutes to get to the bakery before they sell out."

"Then we won't be having lunch together."

Evelyn stepped from the table to the counter where her black leather handbag sat. "What are *your* plans?"

"I'm going to the library again. I was given some suggestions for books to read with good examples of style I might follow."

"Do whatever helps," Evelyn said as she plucked her vehicle key fob from the handbag. "I'm on my way. Wish me luck." She disappeared into the garage, leaving him to stare at the artificial holiday greenery over the door. What swap meet was she talking about?

He heard the familiar rumble of Evelyn's car as she headed out. The sound faded away. He leaned forward to look out the window to make sure she didn't suddenly do a turnaround to recover something she left on the counter. The street remained empty except for a man and woman walking an Irish wolfhound.

Now that he was alone, he shifted his attention to the cream-colored telephone sitting on the desk. The honking of a Canada goose from the bird clock on the wall announced that it was ten. Alice should be long finished with having breakfast and washing the dishes.

He picked up the handset and punched in two digits and stopped, concentrating. The numbers were not coming. Unbelievable! His mind had reached the point where he couldn't even remember how to call his sister! He reached across and spun the Rolodex; under "A" was the smudged listing for "Alice." He slowly and carefully pressed each of the numerals. There was a ring.

A very familiar voice said, "Yes, who's there?"

"This is your big brother, Steve. Remember?"

"Well, how are you, stranger?"

"I'm doing fine, except I'm a little older than the last time I called."

She scolded him, playfully. "I should say so. How many months has it been? I was beginning to wonder if you had died."

"I know it's been a while, sis, but nothing new ever happens here for me to call about. I do think about you though. What's new with you?"

"I just recovered from a bout with shingles. But you didn't call me to ask me that. Were you looking for some sisterly advice? It's free."

As he was about to speak, he visualized the address book lying in the box in the garage. He should have brought it to the phone. There were names there he needed to ask about.

"In a way," he said. "I happened to be going through that box of dad's stuff you sent me. I looked at a few of his effects, some awards, some keepsakes, the usual things that he treasured, but I got curious about the history of some of the pieces in his collection. I thought you might know the background. You used to talk to him a lot."

"I tried, but he would shrug off some of my questions. What caught your interest?"

"There was an airbase newspaper in the box. I began thinking about dad's job during the war as chief inspector for the air field. I know you were just a teenager like me at the time. Did he ever talk much about his job?"

"Like what?"

"Did he ever tell you anything about the people he worked with. You know, the men and women he supervised?"

"What brought up that question?"

"In the newspaper you sent there was a photo of him receiving recognition for his good work. There was an impressive-looking group of people standing next to him."

"I know. I saw the photo."

"Did he ever get to know them personally?"

"How do you mean?"

"Did you ever hear him talk about any of his people? I wondered if he became a close friend with any of them. Do you know if he ever visited them or called them?"

"I don't know how dad spent his time, and I never listened to his phone calls. Why does that matter to you?

"I was talking to Evelyn the other morning about how I wasted many opportunities to talk to dad about his work, to show him I was interested in what he was doing during the war. The few tales he did tell me did gave me a little insight into the nature of his job. But I was young, and my mind was on other things: finding a part-time job, girlfriends."

Alice's tone became very cheerful. "He loved what he was doing. I do remember him telling me at an earlier time how his job at the truck body company was shaky, he worried he might be laid off—with no prospects for work. Then the war broke out, and he found employment at the airfield that lasted the rest of his life."

Somewhat glum, Steve said, "It was the same with me, Alice. Dad never burdened me with the full story about his money problems, but I knew he had them. Businesses were still recovering from the depression when we were growing up. The guy that dad worked for, Eldon Krime, was fighting hard to keep the truck company afloat. Sometimes he couldn't meet the salary deadlines. Dad joked that a saying started going around the shop: *Krime doesn't pay.*"

Steve waited to hear her chuckle, but the line was silent. He continued. "The war was terrible, Alice, but it rescued dad."

Alice sounded more sober. "That inspector position wasn't easy though, Steve. It was hard, sometimes dirty work. I remember seeing him come home exhausted, way past his regular quitting time, too tired to eat a decent dinner. He was under a lot of pressure and had a lot of responsibility. He spent many days, often during intense heatwaves, making notes inside shot-up bombers that were flown in from overseas. He told me they were in bad condition. He said he could imagine what it must have been like for the crew during bombing raids, with enemy fighters and flak coming at them. He said many of the planes had the strong smell of urine."

"Well, the caption under the picture in the paper said the people on his team really looked up to him. I wondered if they got to know him well. You know—took him out to dinner, visited at the house."

"Nope. Never saw anyone come to the house."

"I looked in the address book that was in the box," he said. "I think some of the names were for people in the photo. Did he ever mention a Loren being in his group?"

"Never heard the name Loren."

"How about Marty Belchef?"

"I don't recognize the last name, but he did mention a Marty once." She began to sound impatient. "I have to ask, Steve, what good is all this digging?"

"A few of those guys in the photo were a lot younger than dad. Some of them could still be alive and kicking. I might give them a call. I think they will understand."

"As I said, Steve. None of those people you mention every dropped by the house—as far as I know."

"Any phone calls?"

"Let me think. There was one afternoon when I got home from school. Yeah. Dad had taken the day off from work and was away somewhere, getting his car fixed—I think. The phone rang; I picked it up. It was a woman. She apologized for calling, but said that she was at the airbase and needed to speak to him. It was an urgent matter. She didn't say what."

"Did she give her name?"

"She probably did. God, that was over fifty years ago, Steve. I don't remember."

"Did he ever mention a Bernice?"

"No, and that wasn't the name of the woman that called, if you're hoping to prompt my memory."

The sight through the window of Evelyn's car rolling up the driveway surprised him. She said she would be gone the rest of the afternoon. It would be wise to wrap up the phone call. Anyway, he had exhausted his questions for Alice. He said hurriedly, "Evy just came home, Alice. She may need my help. I'm going to sign off.

"Okay, Steve, take care. And by the way, thanks for the birthday card." The line went dead.

Evelyn's voice came from the kitchen. "I'm home, sweety."

He joined her at the refrigerator where she was shoving beer cans, sauce bottles and plastic food containers aside to make room for a large pink carton.

"It has a whipped cream frosting," she said. "It has to be kept cold. I'm leaving again, dear, for more food. Now's a good time to go if you have any errands yourself."

"Yes, I do. I have to make another trip to the library."

Evelyn headed for the front door. Steve followed.

The parking at the library was light. He found a spot close to the entrance. There was a new announcement mounted on the easel in the courtyard, but he didn't stop to read it. He forged in, heading straight for the reference desk.

Fortunately, Miss Wilkins was at her workspace with no line of people waiting to ask questions of her. He walked up and leaned on the counter.

"You may remember me," he said with confidence.

She squinted, smiled weakly, her head pivoting slowly as she tried to place him.

He continued in a positive manner. "It was back in September. You suggested a book I should check out and study in connection with writing biographical material. The title was something about memories recalled."

She stared blankly for a few seconds, then her eyes relaxed as she connected with him and his question. She touched her forehead. "It's coming back. The book you're referring to is *Precious Moments Recalled.* It's a collection of short stories by noted women prose stylists. I don't think they've been given enough recognition; I consider them in the same league with Jane Austen. You could learn something from them."

"Where do I find it?"

She started tapping on the keyboard. "I'll give you a number, but you'll want to search by author's names too. Let's see, look for Elaine Tellwegger, Bernice Batelle, and Marie Osterford."

Her words were a punch to his head. He was surprised and embarrassed by the volume of his voice as he came back at her sharply. "*What* did you just say?"

She was startled. "Marie Osterford," she repeated.

"No, no." His hand violently fanned the air between them. "The second author."

"Bernice Batelle."

There was rising tension in his chest. He heard the name correctly; he wouldn't ask her to repeat it. Between some heavy breaths he spoke somewhat grittily. "Okay, where will that book be?"

She started tapping the keyboard again. "Oh, oh, it's checked out. Would you like me to place a hold on it?"

"No. Do you have any other books or stories by that Batelle you mentioned?"

"No, I wish we did. About eight months ago I read in the book review section of the newspaper that she had started a new novel long ago, but her publisher has never made any announcement yet of a pending release. I was really looking forward to reading it. One of our library patrons told me she wasn't able to finish it."

"How would they know?"

"They may have asked her. She's a local author."

"A *local* author?"

"Yes. She lives here in Springfield. I've heard she visits the library a lot. She did a book-signing here, down the hall, quite a few years ago. Although I have never met her."

His ears went up. "Lives here in Springfield" were the words he clearly heard. He began thinking of ways to phrase the obvious question without *being* obvious. "Is it possible for people who admire her work to pay her a visit?" he asked.

"Yes." She recovered her small white pad and began jotting. "Here's an address for her I was given. It's a little old; she may have moved." She handed Steve the slip.

He folded the paper without looking at it, mumbled, "Thanks for the information," and began walking very slowly, his mind not yet able to come to grips with what he had just heard.

FINAL TRYST

STANDING in the sunlight that filtered through the trees in the library courtyard, Steve examined the small square of paper given to him a few minutes ago, the rude wind flapping it, pulling it from his hand as he tried to make out the street name where somebody named "Batelle" lived.

He should have pressured Miss Wilkins a little more to explain, when *exactly*, she was given this address. She admitted it was old; that could have been ten years ago. Houses change hands more often than that. Attempting to find the place and a specific person could be a fool's errand. Then again, what would be the harm in just driving by? Maybe he might see the woman in question standing on her front porch or checking her mailbox.

He rubbed the paper with his thumb, as if, by the mere motion, he could divine the details of this mystery. This connection, this new turn of events, required some thinking, some sorting out. The afternoon had begun as a simple, pleasant trip to the library to ask about a book. Now he had been thrown into a state of total unrest, compelled to come to grips with the fact that there was possibly a woman, somewhere out there, with the same name given to him in a dream. It could be a coincidence.

A handful of people, some old, some young, bundled up for the winter weather, some carrying totes with books, marched past him in the walkway, in and out of the library. They smiled and greeted one another, looking to be in good holiday spirits. Unfortunately, he was not; his mind was occupied with the prospect of a frantic, agitated search for a house with an address that may not even be correct.

Reason suggested there was probably a simple and logical explanation for what was going on here. If so, it was uncomfortable to admit his aging brain cells had forgotten the circumstances that tied him to this mystery woman. The clues were there: the book title scrawled on the edge of the airbase newspaper seemed to indicate his father knew about a book with stories written by a woman named Batelle. The photo indicated his father knew a woman who was a dead-ringer for Bernice.

He remembered, vaguely, when he was a teenager, his father reciting little anecdotes about his work as an airbase inspector during World War II, stories about the ironic or exceptional things he and his team did to keep bombers flying. Yes, it *was* possible that his father had told him about a woman that reported to him, a memory that evaporated like so many others.

The day his father brought the airbase newspaper home he may have pointed out, with great pride, the front-page photograph that included, clearly visible, the woman that resembled Bernice. It may have made an impression on him, but the viewing had never occupied his mind again until now. Had the image of that woman arisen from deep within his subconscious by way of his dreams?

He needed some answers. He stepped over the curb, walked the twenty-five feet to his car, and got in. With no other moving vehicles in view, he backed out abruptly, shifted into drive energetically, and headed, with determination, into the traffic of the city avenues.

As he sped along, it was difficult to read the narrow street signs atop the thin, black poles at the intersections. Finding the address may not be that easy. Besides, he was fighting the temptation to just turn around and head home—and he was losing that fight. This playing detective was childish and unnecessary. He steered toward the curb, braked to a stop, cut the engine, rolled his window down, and took a deep breath.

The cold, December afternoon air brushed his cheek. He slumped back against the seat, an attempt at relaxation, but it was not to be had. He kept asking himself about all the ways this might end.

And there was Evelyn to think about. She will be wondering where he was. How will he explain this trip when he got home? He could say he was referred to this "Bernice", a "very professional, experienced guide" to spinning memories in print. But that might be stretching the truth a little. And besides, that bridge might not have to be crossed; there may be no woman by that name where he was headed.

What *was* that address? From his breast pocket he fished out the small paper again, unfolded it, and looked at the numbers: *2502 South Grove Avenue.* The street name sounded familiar, but it was in a part of Springfield he had never visited. In the glove compartment he found a well-worn street map, opened it, spread it over the passenger seat, and studied the index of street names. Grove Avenue was five blocks ahead. He started the car and rolled forward.

As he entered the neighborhood indicated by the street guide, a tall light standard appeared. At the top, a green metal plate displayed the name Grove in white letters. He turned right; the street was empty. The grassy parkways on either side held rows of thick, evergreen trees that blocked his view of the houses. He stopped the car, again taking a quick look down at the circled area on the map. He let the car creep forward as he peered out of the windshield, attempting to decipher house numbers on the curb; most were worn away. He pulled to the side and stopped the car again.

He began to question the sense of the hunt. If the woman he sought actually lived somewhere ahead, what did he plan to do? Knock on her door? Will there be a husband, a Mr. Batelle, answering the knock, waiting for an explanation? What was his excuse for calling on her? Then again, *she* might answer the door. He envisioned himself standing in front of woman with a puzzled look while he was grasping at words.

The imagined outcomes were getting to be unreal. Was he about to tell a total stranger that he had dreams about her? Was it even conceivable that a person could visit another person in their sleep? Would she know him when she opened her front door?

If she had worked with his father, Arthur may have told her about his son, Steven. In that event, was he bold enough to say, "Hello, I'm Arthur Ribman's son; perhaps you know of me?" But *could* she have worked with his father during the war? That was long ago. She would now be a human relic in her nineties, not the energetic, aware woman of his dreams, not the woman who kissed him.

Who was she—really? And what was his connection to her? Where, in the dim past, could he have heard the name "Batelle?" Perhaps an English teacher had assigned the class to read a story by Bernice Batelle. Then again, maybe it *wasn't* Bernice, maybe it was Bernadette something. He didn't remember that either, but the name must have remained buried somewhere in his brain. The dreams merely dredged up the face of a woman, and a name, and pasted them together. Then the woman in his dream was not really Bernice Batelle.

He could sense that his anxiety and the chatter of his thoughts were dangerously impairing his attention to the traffic in the cross streets, to people stepping out from the curb, to careless drivers swinging open their car doors inches close as he passed. This mission wasn't worth an accident. He pulled to the side again, and parked.

This puzzle surely had an obvious solution; he was making too big a deal of it. He had all the bits and pieces; he was not connecting them properly. Sitting stock still, staring up through the windshield at the tree over the car, he constructed the most sensible scenario. This was how it went: his father had shown him the photograph in the airbase newspaper years ago. He probably even pointed out each of the men and women in his team that were pictured. Yes, the attractive woman in the photograph, the woman that later occupied his dreams, had caught his attention. And yes, the English reading assignment made sense. The teacher had mentioned "Bernice Batelle" to make the class aware of the range of prose styles. That was it. His subconscious had simply combined the name and the face and, by way of his dreams, offered up this imaginary woman who handed him the solution to stringing words together. That made sense, but still, the burning need to know who lived at the house on South Grove Avenue overrode his logic.

He passed rows of homes looking very much alike except for the owners' choices of colors and decorative plants. The few mail box numbers he could make out told him he was very close to ground zero. He slowed as he approached a large parking area.

As he rolled past a pair of tall willow trees blocking his line of sight, a bold, bright, two-story structure came into view against the dark blue sky. It was obviously not a home, more of an office building. Clearly visible at the top right corner, large numerals in sharp black said 2502.

This had to be the place. The building had a rough, white exterior and yellow-trimmed windows. As he entered the driveway, several parking slots popped into view at his left. He eased into one, removed the ignition key, stepped out, and locked the door.

He took the narrow walkway that led to a wide, glass-paneled entrance. Above the door were large, silvery metal letters that spelled out SENIOR OASIS. He looked up at the words twice, puzzled. This was not a home or an apartment house, more like some kind of business. He looked again at his note, frowning. The address matched.

He pushed open the door and stepped into an anteroom; it was cool, quiet, and dimly lit by small bulbs in the ceiling. The single person at the entrance desk was a woman facing the wall, talking on the telephone. She heard his steps, replaced the handset, and came about as he entered. The white jacket she wore had blue trim on the collar, sleeves and pockets—like a hospital uniform. She placed her knuckles on the counter, and faced him. She said softly, "Good afternoon."

For a moment he was distracted by a white badge on her jacket with blue script that read *Hi, I'm Margot.* He cleared his throat. "My name is Steven Ribman."

"Well, good afternoon Mr. Ribman, What can I do for you?"

"I'm looking for a Bernice Batelle. I was given this address for her. Does she work here?

The receptionist stiffened slightly, frowned, then smiled. "No. She's a resident here."

"A resident?"

"Yes."

"Is this a medical facility? Is she ill?"

"This is Senior Oasis, an assisted living home. She is being cared for here."

He could see he had to change his line of questioning. He tried to make his voice apologetic. "From what I know of miss Batelle I didn't expect to find her to be in place like this."

She smiled. "Well, you're not the first person to be surprised. I should introduce myself. I'm Margot Endenstoke, I'm the senior assistant to the administrator here. I'm very familiar with all the residents."

"Then you could put me in touch with her?"

"I assume you're asking about Phyllis."

Things were coming too fast. The word "Phyllis" jarred him; tension raced through him. Wait, that was the name Bernice told him to use for the woman in his book; that was a different person. Things were coming apart. He waved the small paper nervously and repeated what he said earlier, "I'm looking for a Bernice Batelle."

"She's here. But that's her pseudonym—her pen name. Most people don't know that. She's famous here. We're really proud of her and her writings. Are you a relative?"

He hadn't planned on this. His words will have to be chosen even more carefully. This Margot may be confused, but he will go along with what she was trying to tell him. "Her writings . . . yes, her writings. I'm a great admirer of her work. I had hoped to meet her and ask for some professional advice."

"Well, let's go find her."

"I don't want to disturb her if she's tied up."

"You won't. I think she's right over there in the Community Room."

Margot turned and walked through a wide archway into a high-ceilinged, spacious area, lit by the reflected sunlight. Steve followed, taking note of the many sofas and armchairs occupied by elderly men and women. Some were looking at each other, chatting. Some simply stared ahead. Off to the side was a Christmas tree decorated with small red, green, and silver globes and a few strings of tinsel.

Margot pointed toward an extremely large window, almost floor to ceiling, that opened upon a garden at the rear of the building, a garden arranged with short and tall dormant bushes, a small pool, and a fountain in the middle that erupted intermittently with a weak pulse of water.

"There's Phyllis," she said, "Phyllis McKardle. She likes to watch the birds bathe in the fountain among the flowers. She loves them. Except there aren't too many birds this time of year. And not many flowers either."

Again, the name she spoke rang in his ear. Steve turned toward the silhouette where her finger pointed. A man was holding up a newspaper, partially blocking his view. Behind the man was the head and shoulders of a very old woman sitting close to the large window, almost touching the glass.

Her head turned his way slightly, and for a moment he felt the urge to about-face and walk quickly away. But she was unaware of anything other than a large bird that had landed on the edge of the pool and was dipping its beak in the water.

He studied the few features he could see of her face. It was much, much older than that of Bernice in his dreams, but it was *her*. Yes, the shape of the eyes, the length of the nose, the curve of the jaw.

He commented, "She looks very old."

"She's ninety."

His growing bewilderment rose, altering his expression. "I can't imagine a person her age doing much creative writing."

Margot began explaining. "No, she hasn't written anything for a long, long while. She told us some time ago she had plans for a whole novel based on her life. This summer a relative bought a laptop computer for her to use. She tried, but her arthritis— in her hands, you know—too painful."

Margot held her hands up to Steve's chest, balling and opening them several times to demonstrate Phyllis's condition, her face tightened as if in agony.

She hesitated, then spoke again. "As foolish as it might sound, mister Ribman, I volunteered to let her dictate to me. That didn't work out. I'm not a speedy typist. I couldn't keep up."

"Not many people could," he said.

"So, then I tried having her simply relate those happy and sorry hours of her life while I patiently listened."

Steve began thinking of some ruse to have Margot share a little of what Phyllis had told her. He said, "I imagine her rundown on day-to-day life was sometimes trying for you."

Margot's pitch went up as she answered. "No, actually her stories are really interesting and they carry a lot of feeling. However, I was expected to compose the narrative that captured the agony or the thrill of it all."

He thought about his own struggle with words. He wanted very, very much, to know exactly what Margot heard from her, and how she handled her stories, but he backed off and only concluded, "She put a lot of trust in you."

Margo said sadly, "That didn't work either. I have absolutely no literary gifts. I had to beg off from helping her. But Phyllis didn't complain. She took my hand, thanked me, and said she will find an author somewhere to help her."

Margot's last words forced Steve to re-think his understandings of what was happening. *Phyllis will find an author somewhere.* How did this woman, seated across the room from where he stood, come to be involved in his dreams, his life?

Was *he* the author she found? Or was she dreaming also? The evidence indicated she knew his father well, perhaps too well. He thought about the kiss. Was he filling in for his father? The answers to all his questions might be as simple as walking up to her and asking outright: Did you know my father? Do we know each other? But he could not bring himself to do that.

He asked, "What did she do to find help with her writing?"

"I'll never know. Something good must have happened. In the last few months, she hasn't fretted to me once about failing to get her story told before, as she puts it, she 'sloughs off this mortal coil.' Somehow she has found peace."

He watched for some behavior by the mystery woman scanning the sky for birds, but she sat as unmoving as a statue. "She seems so immobile. Does she ever get out much?"

"For sure. Every now and then she will ask one of our attendants to take her to the library, or a book store. She's an avid reader. And loves to go out for coffee."

More questions began to form in Steve's mind. "Did she ever tell you what she did in her life. I mean, did she have another career besides writing?"

"Oh, yes. Her writing was just a sideline. A good portion of her career was spent at the airfield."

"Airfield?"

"She was a technical writer at a company that manufactured airplane hardware. When world war two broke out, the airfield snapped her up at almost twice the salary. She told me she spent a lot of time crawling in and out of airplanes, and a lot of time on the phone with suppliers."

Steve became rigid, absorbing Margot's words, overwhelmed by what she was saying. Why should he be surprised? He should have known all that from what he had heard in his dream and saw in the newsletter in the past weeks.

"Would you like to say hello to her? Do you want me to introduce you?"

"No, now that I understand her condition, I might be imposing."

Steve accepted that the woman in the chair, patiently surveying the few bushes outside the window was to be known as Phyllis. "She seems very quiet," he commented. Does she avoid socializing with the other people?"

"No. She likes to talk a lot. Well, to anyone who will listen to her. I do. I find her interesting. She has written some poetry. However, that's not her strong suit."

Margot put her fingers to her chin and thought a moment. "She might appreciate the visit from you. She has had almost no visitors. She told me all her friends have died. We often sit together. She tells me stories about her mother and her father."

He had an image of Margot having tea with Phyllis, leaning forward from one of the plush chairs, showing keen interest. If Margot came across his book, she might wonder how all those same stories ended up there.

His tone became resolute and positive. "Well, I'm glad to know she's well-taken care of."

A young man in dark blue scrubs entered carrying a tumbler of some liquid which he gave to a man near the window. Phyllis waved to the young man. He stepped over to her quickly, bent down, and listened. She said a few words and he answered.

Margot caught the interchange, waved at the young man, and said softly, "Clark." The attendant caught the sound of his name, patted Phyllis's hand, and hurried to Margot.

"What does she need?" Margot asked. The young man, Clark, whispered something. Margot turned to Steve. "Phyllis wants to return to her room,

Mr. Ribman. Did you want to say anything before she leaves?"

"No," he said, with some uncertainty in his voice.

Margot turned to the young man, "You can proceed."

The attendant walked back and took a position behind Phyllis and put his hands at the back of where she sat. He pushed and she glided forward a few feet, coming into Steve's view. She was in a wheelchair. The chair had light blue wheels; the fabric on the back was gray with bright pink poppies. Yes, he had seen that combination of colors once before. It was the chair that had almost run him over in The Select Cup four months ago. That was obviously when she sat watching doctor Dohlstram and him, listening to their conversation as they drank their coffee.

Phyllis reached back and touched the attendant's arm. He brought the chair to a stop. Phyllis leaned forward to say a word to someone nearby.

Steve knew he stood at the threshold of possibly more discoveries, facts that could be as distressing as enlightening. He looked at Phyllis feebly gesturing as she shared another story from her past with an equally old woman. An opportunity was at hand—now—to cast more light on this riddle. All he had to do was speak with her. But something held him back.

Was it possible for her to have reached out to him in his dreams—to help him to help her? That only happens in B movies. Maybe he should have spent the twenty-five dollars on the call to Madame Lasseur, the dream consultant.

Then again, what are the odds that this all happened by chance? Could he become aware of this woman from a single photograph, a woman who knew and worked alongside his father, who reached out for someone to document the fragments of her existence, who lives here in Springfield? Was it a coincidence she visited The Select Cup that afternoon?

"I have to be heading out," he said to Margot, turning toward the entryway. He had to put all this behind him. He had to cut all ties to this woman. If he were to allow any relationship with Phyllis to be formed, even a "professional" one, he could expect future calls from her to his home, or even—God forbid—a visit? That would be unexplainable to Evelyn.

Besides, Phyllis herself would want it that way. Didn't she tell him at the cemetery that their meeting was the last? He flattered himself by thinking she saw him as a recovered love. No. All she wanted out of him was a book that highlights the ups and downs in the life of Phyllis McKardle. And that had been accomplished.

Margot raised her voice slightly as he reached the archway. "Would you like me to tell her you stopped by?"

Steve, halted, swung around at her question to face her. His eyes swept across the large room full of people whose lives were running out. He took one more, long look at Phyllis seated near the window, at the flickering, reflected sunlight on her beautiful face, rays bouncing off the fountain. He took one more glance at the chair with the blue wheels and pink poppies.

"No," he said to Margot. "That might start her wondering." He added, smiling, "I'm sure she has enough to think about."

Steve took another step and stopped again, thought hard for a moment and said to Margot, "You might suggest to Phyllis that on her next trip to the bookstore she ask for a new novel about memories that just came out—the title is *Old Songs Are the Best.*"

www.ingramcontent.com/pod-product-compliance
Lightning Source LLC
Chambersburg PA
CBHW070101260626
47160CB00004B/1273